I0822327

GOD'S GRACE ON SUNDAY

Tiese

 This is a work of fiction. Names, characters, places, and incidents either are the product of the author's imagination or are used fictitiously. Any resemblance to actual persons, living or dead, events, or locales is entirely coincidental.

ISBN : 979-8-218-45713-6

There truly is grace for it all, in the name of Jesus.

A story of love, justice, redemption, and obedience,
all while honoring God.

"And God is able to make all Grace abound toward you;
that ye, always having all sufficiency in all things,
may abound to every good work."

2 Corinthians 9:8

Table of Contents

CHAPTER 1
A New Sunday

I'm sticking to the truth. The only truth, and that is God, is the way, the truth, and the light.

I know God sees His faithful servant in me. He knows my heart as I seek to know His, even in all my wrongdoing.

Purity and abstinence have been my journey, and I wasn't going to let any guy ruin what God put as a passion inside of me.

And I wasn't going to let any job rejection define me when God clearly says I'm a masterpiece.

I asked for confirmation after confirmation, for God to tell me if Marcus was the one. I knew he couldn't wait till marriage to have sex like I was, but I still forgave him every time he stepped out on me and then wanted to come back in.

I thought if I forgave him, he would change. We wouldn't be virgins on our wedding night together, but at least he apologized and stuck by me. Until he didn't, and then I would let him back in again.

Marcus was becoming more of a risk to my aligned future with God, and he was blurring my vision, my 'why,' to what I was waiting for.

Most of the time, he didn't have the same values. I tried to press my love of God on him because who wouldn't love God, right?

But I knew I couldn't take the chance anymore. Even though it has been three months since we separated, he still wanders through my mind and through texts on my phone. But two days after my birthday, he texted me a happy birthday, confirming that he wasn't the one.

I knew it was God telling me to move on and that Marcus had a different route than me.

My first love, or what I thought was love, ouch!

I waited through all the affairs and backsliding. If you're truly living for God, there should be no toxic relationship. But I take responsibility for what I allowed, given how much I wanted it to work with him.

Even forgiving him that night, we almost went all the way.

I have set my flesh down and allowed the spirit to work through me, but that night, my legs were almost open, and my mind was shut. But over all of Marcus's sweet words in my ear, his strong hands holding me, and his lips kissing me, I still heard God's voice saying, "You're my child; any promise you make with Me will be more rewarding than what you think Marcus could give you." So, I got up.

I am thankful to still hear His voice through it all. I was redeemed, and that was the last night I was with Marcus. He would bring me flowers, but he saw I wasn't budging. Then he slowly stopped doing that, leading to texting often, to texts a couple times a week, and to a late birthday text.

I took my final confirmation from God so He could start working on something new in me and continue with the plan for my life.

"Thanks, but it was two days ago," I responded an hour later to Marcus's late birthday text.

"Ohh fuck I'm sorry. I went out of town with Dylan and Jason. Time slipped my mind, and we've been checking out the town; I haven't looked at my calendar." He responded 30 minutes later.

I felt my emotions trying to work out a response. I wanted to know why you went without telling me. Where did you go? Why did you go with Jason and Dylan? They encourage worldly behavior and excessive drinking. And I really wanted to know: how, after all these years, you forgot my birthday and must revert to a calendar?

But instead, I let God's peace speak through me.

And I knew it was over.

"It's cool. Have a good trip." There was nothing there, and I knew what he wanted. I just wasn't going to give it to him. I wanted to be married in love, approved by God. Marcus wanted to feel experienced and see things because, like he said, "I don't want to miss out."

Although I always wanted to question that statement because I know you could never miss out if God is ordering your steps, he felt differently.

He'd rather be out all Saturday until early Sunday morning, missing church. He was too busy to participate in prayer groups and Bible study. But I always still hoped.

I let go, the pressure fell, and I could go back to being glad of the person being reflected in me in the mirror.

That's me; I'm a whole new Sunday.

Sunday Suddrom.

CHAPTER 2
True Crime to Life

Looking in the mirror, home alone after reading that last text, I saw the relief.

I put my phone down and prayed.

"Thank You, God, for Your guidance and love. I will continue to trust You through the pruning of my life. Amen"

I went to the kitchen to make a turkey sandwich.

I was used to living alone since I agreed not to move in with a man until I was married.

I tried it before with Marcus, but so many times, it became a risk to almost have sex.

I try not to let Marcus be the reason for everything; I really do like living alone.

Then Ashley Montgomery, my greatest friend, and I considered moving in together, but she wanted to live with her boyfriend, Nick Apollo; she's happy there.

I have been able to afford this small apartment due to my grandfather's inheritance. I used some of the inheritance to get my teaching master's degree for elementary students, and the rest has been useful for living as I find a job.

When my sister, April, was living with me, she would help with a good part of all the bills and rent. She was well off; she makes production sets for movies, so her part of the inheritance was more like a big savings.

The apartment was one bedroom, but I managed on the couch, and we shared a pretty big closet space.

Then she got a job in Texas and met a guy, and they have been engaged for almost a year now.

When she moved out, I got a brand new bedroom set with all the essentials and finally had my room.

As long as I'm moving toward something, taking care of myself is manageable. It's my 25th birthday, and I think of how far I've come and all the hopes I set, seeing some come to pass and the rest I still believe for.

My keynote is to always remind myself to "trust God's timing."

I'm glad to just be enjoying my turkey sandwich today.

I celebrated my birthday with Ashley and Nick, my sister; April flew out with her man, Harlem. My parents came from Berkeley, which was about 5 hour drive from me, with my sweet grandma, and we ate really good food with great desserts, and I was blessed with many gifts.

Everyone is home, and I still have cake.

I can now enjoy my turkey sandwich and my show, Dateline.

Getting back to my rhythm and settling for the day on the couch.

Before Dateline came on, the last news report broadcasted on TV.

News reporter: 22-year-old Rebecca Meyers has been missing for two weeks now. Friends said she drove off from a house party Saturday night after wanting to go home. Her boyfriend would be coming to see her in the morning after visiting family in a different state. Although her friends told her it wasn't good for her to drive after heavy drinking, she left anyway. Her mother said she came home that night disoriented and panicked and said she did something very bad. Her mother believed her to be just highly under the influence, needing some rest, and disregarded her statements. Until four days later, she goes missing late that Wednesday night, after her mother said Rebecca received many phone calls and notifications, putting her on high alert. Rebecca then told her mother she would be back and had an errand to take care of, got in her car, and never returned home. A week later, her car was found on the side of a road with all her belongings, such as her purse, wallet, and keys, but no phone. Investigators are searching further into her lifestyle, her boyfriend, and the huge dent on the right side of the front end of her car. If anyone has any leads, information, or answers, please contact the local sheriff's department. Rebecca's family is anxiously waiting. And if you are interested in helping search for Rebecca, there will be a local meeting spot for everyone to gather and then disperse among the area where her car was found and the surrounding areas. Thank you.

The story struck me, and I instantly wanted to learn more. It was so close to home; the girl was young. I felt it to be stewardship, being in God's kingdom, searching for lost children, literally and figuratively. Plus, I love true crime stories.

For the rest of my evening, I became a true crime detective, seeking information on the Rebecca Meyers case and how I could help.

CHAPTER 3
The Field

"Wow, Sunday, you really looked through all this information on Rebecca Meyers?" Ashley asked me as she saw the folder page I created for the investigation on my laptop.

Ashley and I were at our local coffee shop. We support small black businesses, and the owners were siblings who love coffee, people, and God—my kind of shop.

We were usual Starbucks girls, but this shop offered homemade coffee beans and teas made from the Jamaican islands.

"Yes, Ash, it's so sad, and nothing adds up. This is one of those cases where one specific person knows something but refuses to speak up." I say it with sternness.

"So, they need people on this who care and are willing to do their own investigations." I continue.

"Isn't that the opposite of what they say—don't do your own crime-solving?" Ashley said.

"That's for family members sake. Their emotions rock the case. I'm a concerned Samaritan." I said this while turning my computer back around to face me.

Danny, one of the owners, served us our drinks. I ordered a mocha frap to attend to the warm California day, and Ashley got her coffee expresso.

"So will this be your hobby till you hear back from Sunrise Elementary School?" Ashley asks while sipping her coffee.

Sunrise is a Christian elementary school. It's not the nearest to my apartment, but I love their values, so the 45 extra minutes would be worth it.

I'm on the hiring waitlist.

"I guess. I submitted everything on time, with high scores and passionate interviews. I have one last one, which is the group interview. I'm just waiting for them to call a date for that." I explained it to her.

"And I don't like group interviews; last time I had one, I felt people were building off my answers. I understand how that setting works for educational purposes when creating curriculum with other teachers, but I want a one-on-one session where I can thoroughly explain myself." I say.

"I want to explain why I add value to the school and how my faith will be put into all that I create." I continue to say.

"Just enjoy the frap and have all that faith you urge people to keep." Ashley says this in her mocking tone.

I've been friends with Ashley since the beginning of college—almost seven years. I met her right before I started dating Marcus. She also grew up in a Christian home but never took to her personal relationship with Christ. She enjoyed college parties, trying drugs, and the stage in life where she dated some bad boys. But she soon felt that her college experience was overwhelmed by trying to do everything all at once. Ashley fell behind and graduated a year after me from USC. The plans we made were hindered, and she fell into depression, had a failed relationship, and had a pregnancy scare. Then, when Ashley and her boyfriend, Damien, got back together, more drugs and smoking occurred, and she went into rehab for three months. Damien, however, went into a different rehab and then went off with someone else. She had to commit to the fact that saving her life was more purposeful, which meant staying sober and away from Damien. Letting him go eventually got easier as she dedicated her life to herself and got back on track with God. She started working and then met Nick one day when we were shopping at the mall two years ago. I'm proud of her and her testimony.

I take a sip of my frappe; it's sweet, chilly, and delicious.

Ashley drinks more of her coffee as she scrolls on her phone.

"You texting Nick?' I ask her as I see her smile at her phone.

"Yes, he's telling me about the plans for dinner tonight with his cousin; they're going over more business ideas for Drive Nick. He always tells me how he can't wait to see how pretty I look when we're all dressed up for dinner." She explains.

Drive Nick is Nick's driving service company; he's been working on it since he was 21. His cousin, Ross, is the investor.

Ashley and Nick have that cute thing about them. A lot better than Damian from college; she was chasing these kinds of sweet moments, and now she gets to experience them in peace.

"Aww, he always knows how to make the moments right." I say to her.

"Yes, and cheers to keeping my faith in him." She responds.

We put up our coffees to cheer each other on.

"And don't worry, sis, I'll look out for any worthy bachelors while I'm out." Ashley tells me with a smile.

I've let her search out a guy for me twice; on both occasions, nothing has prospered.

Leaving that in God's hands has become my only option.

"Girl, you better not!" I exclaim to her.

"I need to let things be natural with a will from God." I continue to say.

However, I felt that maybe I would have to get out more.

It's been a bit of a routine to stay home, study for my teaching job, and leave the past of Marcus behind me.

"No, you are way too fine with your beautiful brown skin, big brown eyes, and straight white teeth to let things just be all natural. You're natural enough with big curls and a tight body. You're a catch that needs to be thrown out in the ball field." Ashley remarks with her sass.

"Plus, I know they have to be God-favored; I always make note of it." She adds.

"Wow, girl, it sounds like you are trying to pimp me." I say it jokingly.

"And you know I don't swing or throw myself into fields like that." I continue with hand quotes.

"I'm not in the club scene, and I don't want to demonstrate that behavior. I need the man to know that I'm a godly woman." I say it with assurance.

"I tried both ways with Marcus, and it left me questioning myself too many times." I say.

"I have to know what it is that I want; leave it in God's hands so He can make a path to a relationship for me." I say.

"I believe it will happen enough to not have to run and expose myself in the field." I continue.

Ashley leans in and listens to my every word.

"Well, sometimes taking your light out into the field might change a couple of those players." She says this while finishing the last sip of her coffee.

I sit back, appalled by her comment. It wasn't so far off from being a good thing.

"Nick found me out, still coming down from my wildness in the field." She says.

"And like I say, I have faith in him and thank God for him." Ashley remarks.

"That's really powerful, Ash and I'm happy for you both." I say to her.

We smile at each other.

"Thanks, sis and of course you're always on my "to be thankful for" list to God." She says.

"Thanks, girl, I know, as well as to you." I reply.

"So, let's see what happens when I go out with Nick and his cousin tonight. I'll keep my eyes open." Ashley says.

"Wouldn't that be kind of weird since Nick's cousin Ross kept trying to date me?" I ask while closing my laptop as we get ready to leave.

"He got over it; Nick says he's dating someone. I'm not sure if I'll be meeting her tonight, though." Ashley explains.

I feel grateful for that because I wasn't interested in Ross so much, particularly because he was moving so fast, almost lacking self-control.

Sustaining is my journey all by itself. Focusing on God and His word while the world keeps going on doing worldly things is a process, and I'm always trying to stand firm. Then, having to explain that to people, especially the men I have tried dating, becomes a whole other journey.

But I get that's life, a journey. And the thing about being a child of God is that the journey lasts forever.

The men will even insist on saying, "Let's do it at least once to know how it feels together."

Temptation is its own field from which I refrain.

I understand being fruitful, and I know if I want to get married to experience the satisfying pleasure of sex, I must meet someone first, the right one for me.

God will make the way for an ordained relationship that stands strong on His word—that is more than what physical can offer.

That's truth.

"Ok, let's go, girl. I have more detective work to do, and you have to get ready for your date night." I say as we pick up our trash to leave,

We start to giggle as we walk out and head to her car as she tells me what she plans to wear tonight.

CHAPTER 4
Knowing Rebecca

My morning routine was a bit different today. I kept on with my prayer time and reading God's word, but I didn't meet with my church group like every Friday morning.

I was moved by more information following the Rebecca Meyers case.

I asked for God's forgiveness for missing the group session; I just felt compelled by the new leads.

I have trusted the works of the Holy Spirit in guiding me to do a thing.

I made a breakfast of oatmeal with all kinds of berries, fresh from the local farmers' market, and a boiled egg. Then, I gathered my notepad for the investigation.

I didn't even text Ashley back concerning her date/business meeting night with Nick and his cousin.

She sent me a text asking me to come and join them, but there was no way I would be a part of that 5th wheel situation. I know that Ross is seeing someone now, but he was very fervent about us getting together. I just don't want to add more to that fire.

Plus, I didn't want another lecture from Ashley about how I need to showcase myself more if I want a man. Then, Nick, who often puts in his two senses out of brotherly love, would be going on and on with Ashley about going out.

I need to stay focused just in case the school calls, and going out right now and potentially missing a call is worrisome.

I will turn my attention to the new information about the Meyers girl and stay home from the church group.

Research information: New leads suggest that Rebecca Meyers was involved in a sexual act conspiracy, where a friend of Meyer's said she told her that she was participating in sexual favors in lieu of clearing her name from being involved in drug trading. Her friend, who has asked to remain anonymous for safety, said Meyers started to take shrooms and inhale cocaine while selling it on a regular basis, then asked for help and guidance for the way out. The person(s) she was involved with have not been identified, and she kept her whereabouts silent. She lost her job and school credits. The night she left the party highly intoxicated, she met with her boyfriend, Leo Hanes, who had been arrested, sought for questioning, and will remain in custody until further investigation. He denies any involvement with Meyer's disappearance and said the night he came into town; she was already very anxious and on edge—more than an alcohol reaction. All she could say was that she had made a big mistake that night. Hanes said he never met the main supplier and only got involved to help Rebecca; he had no idea what she was really into. He also said that whatever she did before meeting up with him that night was what sent her down a spiral path for the next few days leading up to her disappearance. Meyer's mother and Leo said she seemed to be jumpy as if someone were looking for her, and that she was under the influence most days. Her disappearance is a mystery, mainly because her secret lifestyle came to light, shocking many who knew her, such as family, friends, and teachers. The main suspect is whomever Rebecca was involved with in the buying, selling, and consumption of drugs. There have been no follow-ups to whom this individual could be. The Meyers family is asking for more help with the local search and information on a possible drug seller in the community. The family also wants you to know that Rebecca was a smart and promising young woman. She was in school to become a veterinarian because of her love of animals. She participated in many clubs on her college campus and had a strong-knit family of mother, father, younger brother, and older sister, as well as her beloved dogs. Rebecca always wanted to help her family, who survived poverty after being in homeless shelters for a year. She continued working at her local buffet restaurant as a waiter. There will be a vigil the night following the first local search for Rebecca. A website in remembrance of Rebecca, has been created in memory of her, and it is open for the public to sign up for the search.

I write down each note in a category section, from most important to least relevant. Starting with the main point, who could the person be that was having Rebecca involved in sexual conspiracies?

I wondered what that entailed—prostitution. No, it couldn't be; they would have said that.

I just don't know a single thing about that lifestyle.

It seems that whoever this one specific person was, the person took advantage of her, trying to advance her by threatening her out of the drug game with sex. Obviously, such sinful and harmful acts result in terrifying consequences.

Also, her turning to drugs and drug sales resulted in the wrong influence coming around when she was probably most vulnerable. If the world's strong social holds hadn't threatened her, I believe she could have achieved great success.

She sounds like a soul I would have loved to bring to Christ because there is, indeed, freedom in Him.

And a lot of the members of the ministry have similar testimonies.

I feel so attached to her—so close.

She was a beautiful young black girl with long box braids and a great smile. She's about 5'5, a college student, and is said to have a great sense of humor.

Someone I could have been friends with.

I wrote down more information about her as I looked at and read more of the testimonies placed by her friends on the website.

I wanted to see Rebecca Meyers remain in the image of who she truly was, not the experience she went through or the mistakes she made. If God forgives her, who is the world to play her for her mistakes?

Although that moment was what took her presence away from her friends and family, it wasn't a definition of what she could have been.

I believe she could have found herself if she had been surrounded by the right crowd.

Hours had gone by. I prayed for her family and her soul, watched more news reports, and read over police reports.

This has consumed me but in a good way. This story reminds me of my blessings. I see myself in this girl, but I was able to find Jesus, my savior. He took the scales off my eyes and showed me the truth.

Which was no Marcus; stop sinning and be a blessing, leading others to Christ.

I follow the world and die or die to my sins and be free in God, where my only job is to keep faith and, of course, follow His commandments.

I get on my knees and thank God for finding me, leaving the 99, and showing me the truth in Him.

Remaining in Him, keeping Him as my source, I am always steadfast in His love.

I crawl up in the fetal position on the floor and weep for God's grace and salvation. He chose me, spared my life, and died for me.

I cried for Rebecca.

"I thank You, God, from the deepest part of my heart." Seeking His presence in this moment.

"God, what can I do now with what I know? How can I bring You glory through this tragedy? Who can I help?"

I realized that this had become my day. It's dinner time, I made a chicken dinner with a side of rice and salad.

I wrote in my prayer journal, took a nice hot bath, and prepared for bed.

I lay restless, tossing and turning. I see that it's a full moon with a clear, dark blue night sky.

"Lord, what must I do with the pull on my heart for Rebecca Meyers?" I whisper.

"How can I serve You with this case?" I whisper once more.

"Who am I called to help?" I ask before I finally feel my eyelids get heavy for sleep.

CHAPTER 5
Moving Heart

I awoke, startled by the sound of my upstairs neighbor's kids playing and jumping around.

I was shocked that I had slept through my alarm.

I wasn't sure if the weight of Rebecca's story or my emotional exhaustion was the cause of my fatigue.

It is the Sabbath, so staying in bed, resting, and meditating on God's word will give Him more honor today, and I will get the rest.

I invested in great bed clothing. Soft, warm-down blankets, a thick cotton-based quilt knitted by my late grandmother on my father's side. I have 1,000 thread-count sheets and pillows filled with heavy-stuffed feathers. My room consists of different shades of warm pink and gray. It is girly; it is me, and spending the day here would be a nice change since I usually enjoy the Sabbath in the living room on the couch.

I felt tired, so I lay back down and softly closed my eyes.

Bang.

The kids go back to jumping around again.

So much for lying in bed with the kids' bedroom right above mine.

There is no school on Saturday, so the kids are home and playing with no hesitation.

I like to believe that everyone knows of God and His commands. And on Sabbath, they all have an easy day and rest. But the world makes up its ideas about Friday evening to Saturday evening, partying, and fornicating.

I will leave it to God to judge. I pray.

I can't believe that my phone hasn't notified me of anything. So, I reach to grab it.

I see that I have multiple notifications from Ashley, my sister, some emails, my news alerts, and a couple of missed calls from unknown numbers.

And my phone was silent for it all.

I instantly think of the teaching job calling me. Although schools are closed on Saturdays, the teacher's administration is open for a couple of hours early on Saturday mornings.

I moved to jump out of bed, but I remembered that I had to pray first.

I get on my knees and *pray, "Our Father, in heaven, hallowed by thy name, Thy kingdom come, thy will be done on earth as is in heaven, Give us this day our daily bread and forgive us of our debts as we forgive our debtors. And do not lead us into temptation, but deliver us from the evil one. For Yours is the kingdom, the power, and the glory forever and ever. Amen.*"

I arise with the feeling of God's peace over me.

And with the hope of receiving good news on the day of rest.

I call one of the numbers back, and the line is picked up.

"Hello, who's calling?" A lady asked.

I stopped to look at my phone in confession; I didn't believe the school secretary would answer the phone in such a way.

"Well, I received a missed call about an hour ago from this number. My name is Sunday Suddrom." I reply.

"Oh, sorry, I believe that someone gave the wrong number for a food order delivery." The person on the other line said:

Ughh.

My heart settles into some disappointment.

"It's okay. Drive safe. God bless." I say, then hang up and walk over to the bathroom.

I use it, then stand to look at myself in the mirror.

Affirmations have always worked.

"I can do all things through Christ, who strengthens me."

I say this to myself ten times in the mirror.

"I'm worthy because God says so."

I say this to myself ten times in the mirror.

"I'm more than a conqueror; I will have purpose and rest today."

I say this to myself ten times in the mirror.

I feel my hunger come over me.

I walk to the kitchen to drink some water before making the call to the other unknown number.

Voicemail picks up.

"Hello, you reached Margret Faizer of the local school teachings of America. Sorry, I missed your call. Please leave your name and number so I can get back to you as soon as possible. Take care. Goodbye."

My heart drops again, this time in shock at finally receiving the call and knowing that I could have missed the opportunity.

"Yes, my name is Sunday Suddrom. I'm returning your call. I look forward to this teaching opportunity and speaking with you. Please call back at 661-555-5784." I say before hanging up.

She obviously has my number if she calls, but I felt compelled to leave it with her.

I hung up, not trying to be consumed by the thoughts and worries.

Then, instantly, I felt that I should have said more in the voicemail about myself, maybe even a short bio.

But I can't be that hard on myself.

I gave my name and number, then spoke into the existence of my excitement to work there.

I put my phone down because it all only works when I leave it to Him.

And, of course, I turned the volume all the way up.

I go make eggs, toast, and avocado.

Now, a call to Ashley.

"Hey girl, how are you?"

I ask nervously. I forgot to reply to her last night and almost forgot this morning.

I just focused on the Rebecca Meyers case all night.

"Why didn't you call me?" She asked with an attitude.

"I was busy researching all the new information on the Rebecca Meyers case." I respond while scrabbling my eggs.

"I'm sorry, girl. Did everything go alright? And I told you I wasn't going to go out." I continue.

"No Ross dropped out of the whole business venture with Nick, and he had a complete meltdown last night." She responds to me in disappointment.

I dropped my spatula.

"Oh, no, what happened?" I ask as I sit down on my kitchen stool.

She takes a deep sigh.

My heart dropped with worry. My heart has been up and down all morning. God, what are You trying to do with me?

"Well, Ross told Nick he found another business venture he thinks would be more beneficial to him and his new girlfriend." Ashley says.

"What is the business venture?" I ask her, confused.

"Makeup! His new girlfriend, Amber, wants to start a makeup line, and she got him to switch sides, just like that on Nick." She said it sadly.

"He didn't get a heads up; no call. He arrived at dinner with Amber, like everything was cool. He ordered dinner, bought us drinks and laughed about something funny their Uncle Steven did. Then he cleared his throat." She continues.

"Amber and I are venturing into the makeup business. I have found with her much research that there will always be a market there because women and men both love makeup and beauty." She says it in a tone mocking his voice.

"No way that is so low. Like he's just going to pull his investment out of the company and drop it all for her makeup company?" I ask.

"Yes, exactly; that's it. It's all she wants. I can tell she was the driving force behind the idea. Ross has never mentioned such a business venture. But she's so materialized and super overdone wearing all that makeup. She completely manipulated him into this." Ashley says.

"She knew Ross was a guy with money and took advantage. She wants to control everything; I can tell by how she sat there like she was the princess at the table, and she owns him. Grinning when he would say how much he loves her and believes in her so much." Ashley continues.

I saw how quick Ross was to change from being a gentleman to a jerk after I turned down his advances and told him it's not ideal to date someone who isn't a follower of God, so I know it's in him to switch up.

"Nick was trying so hard not to get into a loud argument with him at the restaurant, which would have resulted in a fight." Ashley explains.

"We both sat there trying to hold back our anger and from getting loud in that restaurant. While Ross and Amber just sat there amongst one another, unmoved by what we had to say." She says.

"Then Amber had the nerve to speak up and say, 'There is so much growth in beauty that it will always be needed and in high demand. You're more than welcome to join my company; it's called 'Forever Beauty'." She continues.

"And so, I told her, 'That sounds like too much effort to be something that will never be naturally there, and that's true beauty'." Ashley says.

"So, she gets up and tells Ross I'm tired of being disrespected; they never even wished us good luck; even after we invited them to join, it's not our fault the driver's business is going down; let's leave, baby." Ashley says it in a mocking tone.

"Then they threw down some cash to pay for the bill and left." She says.

"He walked off, saying sorry, bro. I hope we can catch up again and talk about how businesses go." Ashley finishes.

"Wow, that's so messed up. Ashley, I'm sorry, girl. I'm sorry for both you and Nick. I know the work and love that were put in by him." I say.

"Yes, girl, so much work, late nights, money gone and crazy marketing. Even the tension it put between the two of us at one point because he put all his time into it. It's like when I finally got to understand what he was building and what it meant for our future, a whole half of it was ripped away from him. Then he's left with paying for the part of the business that was taken out." Ashley says it with sadness.

I feel so bad for my friends.

"I know, girl, we were all so excited for this; we saw all the opportunity it would have." I respond.

"Ya, it really did." She quietly says.

"We're going to look into other avenues; it's just hard to ask for so much money on short notice. But Nick's business plan is phenomenal, and I know he can sell it. He'll get his momentum back." Ashley says it with hope in her tone.

"We stayed and bought more drinks, since he left money to pay for the bill." She says.

"I can tell he took it very hard, girl." Ashley continues.

"I'm sure he did, and I'm here for the both of you." I let her know.

"So please come out with us tonight? You know Nick loves you too and appreciates your encouragement." She pleads.

"Why can't you guys just come over to my place and we can order out or cook?" I ask as I go back to cooking breakfast.

"Because girl, it'll just be dinner somewhere nice, no clubs and you and I need to go out and do something anyway." She responds.

I roll my eyes.

"It's not about finding a guy for you; we just haven't really done anything since, you know, you and Marcus officially spilt." Ashley says.

"Whatever, don't make it about old things with Marcus and me." I quickly reminded her.

"But it is; it's about that and everything else we have gotten through this year. The ups and downs. You have really held it down and remained so good after your breakup, like I knew you would. But I just want to step out and spend time talking about good things with my love and best friend." Ashley explains.

It hit me good. I can enjoy a time out with my friends for dinner. Overcoming so much has been my season. Even the story of Rebecca Meyers has been an extra weight. I trust God with His provision at this time for me. But I'm always tired, at times battling myself about my relationship being strong with God. I'm anxiously waiting for job calls, wanting to help with Rebecca's case, finally feeling released from the curse of being in love with an unbeliever, and all else. It would be nice to go out. God willing.

I put together my breakfast meal and sat down.

"Okay, I'll go out to dinner with you both." I gladly respond.

I heard her scream in excitement. She said she'd call me back after telling Nick the good news.

I prayed over my food.

CHAPTER 6
Savor the Italian

I did take the time to rest all day.

I let go of the worry of the teaching job and put it in God's hands.

I read my appointed scriptures of the Psalms for the day.

I meditated in silence and stillness, seeking to hear God's voice on this beautiful Sabbath day.

I am glad about all that is behind me and what I have learned about myself and my transgression for falling for a non-believer who is obviously more satisfied with himself than who God has called him to be—a difference Marcus could never understand.

And now I understand the curse I have put over myself by putting all the grace God has put on my life into trying to convert Marcus to the truth. Risking my life by almost losing myself in fleshy behavior. Even though I know that act still wouldn't get Marcus to love me or God truly.

I know that a man is supposed to lead, and I was trying to lead his way to Christ, but being unequally yoked is a disaster in itself. Missionary dating, but clearly, I loved the relationship too much.

Officially scraping Marcus out of my life has led me to see the truth and how I wasn't truly following God.

I was battling with the idea that I was a great follower, opening my life to constant spiritual warfare.

Now, I have this new sense of direction. I'm just trying to understand where I'm going and what God wants to do with this new season of my life.

Just being thankful for God's forgiving heart and that He will make all things new.

I have the blessing of great friends, and they need my help and support. Plus, Ashley is right; it's about getting through and through victory, as we are all going through our little battles.

Ashely told me I could pick out the restaurant for dinner tonight.

"Hey girl," I say when Ashley picks up the phone.

"Hey, did you decide on a place? Nick will make the reservations." she asks.

"Yes, Paul's Italiano Bistro." I responded with excitement.

Pasta and wine sound delicious.

"Great! He'll make the reservations for 8 p.m. We're going to start getting ready soon; I'll let you know when we're on the way to get you." She says.

"Okay, I can't wait." I say.

"Me too, bye." She responds.

We hang up, and I have 3 hours till dinner, which is about two and a half hours till they come to get me.

I can take a shower and start getting ready.

What should I wear?

I take a nice hot shower while playing my favorite gospel hits on my playlist.

I step out of the shower and walk to my closet.

My yellow dress instantly catches my eye.

I haven't worn it since going to an old college friend's baby shower a year ago.

I have stayed fit, so I know I can wear it even better than before.

I am wearing my glitter-covered, fashionable sandals. I don't feel like wearing high heels tonight.

I rub my shea butter lotion on my skin and apply my light makeup. Put on my favorite pieces of jewelry. My sparkly gold bracelets and watch. Plus, my dangling glitter earrings.

I rejuvenate my curls, giving each one definition.

My yellow dress has thin straps and fits like a silk glove.

It's not too flashy and tight, but it's respectably complementing.

I grab a small gold purse, and I feel ready and beautiful.

I pray to God to remain in my presence so His laws remain in me, leading to His hand moving over the night. Complete protection from God, mostly to be used for His glory in anything He has planned for my life.

Amen.

I settle in myself.

About 10 minutes later, Ashley texts me.

Ashley: "We'll be there in 10."

Me: "Okay."

I feel a wave of nerves come over me. I told myself that if I felt any bit of this, I shouldn't go, but also, after praying that prayer, I felt there was an assignment by God for me tonight.

And I believe it's to help encourage my friends.

CHAPTER 7
Grand Italian and Beyond

They arrive, and I hear a knock on the door.

"Hey girl, it's me; open up!" Ashley shouts.

I run to meet her at the front door.

I open it, and we instantly grab each other for a hug.

It's nice to see my great friend after the last couple of days we've both been through.

"Nick is down in the truck waiting." She says.

"I just wanted to come up and make sure you were all good before we have dinner together." Ashley says.

"I know we won't have our usual girl time to talk." She explains.

"No, I'm good girl. Thanks, though. I left those worries in God's hands and just want to enjoy my friends as we lift each other's spirits up." I tell her as I grab my coat and purse.

"Okay, great, and you look mighty fine, best friend." Ashley shouts as she grabs my hand, checking me out from my crown to my feet.

"Thank you, and you look beautiful as always, Ash." I say this to her as I blow her a kiss.

My best friend is a beautiful woman, inside and out. I'm so glad she's embracing that now.

"Okay, let's go." We both say it at the same time.

I grab my keys, lock the door, and head down the hallway of the apartment complex till we reach the elevators.

We get in and head straight down, the doors open to the front of the building where Nick is parked.

I think of what I can say to him.

Instantly, the Holy Spirit tells me to start with a prayer.

He gets out of the truck when he notices me and Ashley walking up.

I see he is dressed for the night, looking great in black slacks, loafers, and a button-up grey shirt. Gucci pieces. His style is always clean and sophisticated.

I remember Ashley always thinking it was too much to dress in this attire as often as he does, but she soon found, after cleaning up her style, that it does say a lot about you when you dress ready for the part.

His part was money and corporate business, and since that's her man, Ashley must dress for that too.

So, she wore her red Burberry dress and heels to acquaint herself, which surely matched her man's style.

He walks over and opens her door, then proceeds to open mine.

"Hey Sunday, how are you?" Nick asks.

"I'm great, happy to see you." I instantly reply as I get into his big Chevy truck.

He gives Ashley a small kiss on the cheek before closing the door.

Nick then jumps back in the truck and begins to pull off.

"I'm glad we're going out, you guys, and I'm here for you both. I want to start our night off with a prayer." I began talking.

"Okay, let's do it." Nick pulls over and parks the truck, and we all bow our heads.

Prayer is so powerful, and I'm thankful for friends letting me bring that key gift into our circle more and more.

They are coming to the light.

"Heavenly Father, we thank You for gathering this group of great friends tonight to enjoy a great meal in Your presence. Although hardships have arisen, we trust Your will for our lives. We ask that You bring Nick peace and opportunity for his car business. I ask that You help steward Ashley into being a great Administrator for Nick. I ask that You bring me peace about my job to become a teacher. You have control over all of these things, and we trust You. Let this be a night of peace and laughter, and whatever we can do to get closer to You. In Christ's name, we pray. Amen"

And we all say Amen together.

"Very refreshing; that was a great prayer." Ashley says.

Nick resumes driving, and Ashley plugs her phone in to play music.

She is a devoted Mariah Carrey fan. We know almost every track, especially her older hits.

Thankfully, she plays some old tracks.

"I can't wait to eat and chill out tonight. This will be my night to not think of the business before jumping back in looking for more investors come Monday." Nick says.

Nick is a very hard worker, and he's been at this personal driver business for three years now. He's very smart and went to Howard, where he studied business up until his masters, where he began to work firsthand on building cars. Then, that led to the creation of a personal driver business; he's 28 and full of potential. Has great family values. Very respectful and believes in Christ. This has helped Ashley on her journey with God more than the many years I have tried. He really loves and adores Ashley. He wants her to work for him and to take care of her. And he has always been kind to me, like a little sister.

I trust in his business ethic and believe he can make it out of this sudden demise.

"Yes, me too; let's get this spaghetti on." I say it with excitement.

We laughed, talked, and remained in good spirits for the 35-minute drive to the Italian restaurant.

Thank God for reservations; we instantly see the long line and valet backed up.

Once we're out of the car, we walk up the beautiful entrance of the foyer to the restaurant. It is one of the best in LA.

There are two small waterfalls where couples were taking pictures on either side of the entrance. Where the door stands is a huge glass door that swings open on each side, with a gold handlebar as the knob.

The glass door has carvings that look as if water is streaming down in a crystalized manner.

The walkway, from the beginning of the sidewalk up until the front door, was made of green and blue marble.

The trees were covered and wrapped around with warm lights.

The combination of the scenery, the lights, and the sound of the water made it feel like a sweet escape.

Nick and Ashley walk a little ahead of me, hand in hand, in their stride.

I'm taking in the view and ambiance.

Nick opens the door for both of us and walks to the countertop to tell the lady we are here and ready to eat.

"Isn't this beautiful?" Ashley says this as we both look around.

The inside is made to look like an old Italian place. With brick walls, pictures of old people, and different images that represent Italy. There is a huge waterfall with old, restored gondola boats on the inside. Trees planted on the inside hang down. Small lights above every table keep it lit. It's a dimly lit restaurant that's very pleasant and romantic. Circular wooden tables with small statues as centerpieces. It's got a warm atmosphere, and it smells of delicious food. A man is singing live. You can hear it all throughout the restaurant. He is singing what sounds like romantic Italian music.

I have no idea what he's saying, but the sound of it matched the atmosphere.

His voice over the sounds of the instruments was a beautiful, peaceful melody for dinner.

"Come on, ladies." Nick instructs us to follow behind a female server to our table.

I don't mind being the third wheel here; it's so beautiful, with so many things to look at and admire.

Whenever Nick and Ashley invite me out with them, they always include me in the conversation. I never really felt left out.

We have a great time together, and I'm most thankful for them.

Going through college and meeting people on different occasions, no one remained like these two.

No one could really keep up with my journey being about God, and I so often wanted to do things that stepped out of what I knew was right according to the Lord.

Friendships fell, but what a friend we have in Jesus!

And two great people remained.

Ashley has been through a lot with her addictions and has always found her way of repentance by going back to God.

Nick grew up in a Christian household and kept God a foundation throughout his life. He encouraged Ashley more as they got together, being a good leader. And eventually to her baptism.

It was a beautiful ceremony for us and her family.

I was baptized with my sister when I was 20 years old. Being baptized in the Father, Son, and Holy Spirit was a beautiful ceremony.

I'm so grateful we can sit and pray together and go to church as often as we can. Nick's wild schedule makes some Sundays hard for him, and we share in a great Bible study group of prayer and focus on God and His way.

"Enjoy your food." The lady who led us to our seats said while placing our menus in front of us.

"Thank you." We all said it together with big smiles on our faces.

"This is amazing." I said.

"I can sit here and soak in all of this." Ashley says it with amazement.

"Then do so, babe; no rush; I know one of the investors and food junkies. I'm not sure if he's here tonight, but he told me all about this place; great choice Sunday." Nick says to us.

"Wow, thanks, baby." Ashley says this and leans in to give him a kiss.

"Yes, I appreciate you as well, Nick." I manage to say while they kiss.

The waiter, a young woman, comes over.

"Hello, I'm Samantha. I'll be your waitress for the night. I'm happy to be serving you guys. Please let me start off with some drinks."

She handed us each a drink menu and then went on to tell us about their special drinks, consisting of different wines.

I'm not the biggest drinker; if I do have wine, it's a red Pinot Noir. But I heard her say everything but Pinot Noir; unless she did, I just couldn't understand the combination of her accent and the many options she presented so quickly.

We both looked at Nick. He is the drink guy; even at their home, he has a collection of many wines and liquors.

"Get us all the best Pinot Noir." He tells her.

"Sure thing, of course." She gives us all a nice smile and nods, then walks off.

"The usual, the best. I just can't have too much; there is church in the morning." I say to them.

"Sure thing, we got this." Ashley affirms.

I smile; as long as we are on the same page, the night will go well.

"Yes, it feels good to be out and to enjoy some time without business affairs." Nick explains.

"I'm going to get back to work Monday and speak with some potential investors. They were interested in the business before I just put it all into Ross." He says.

Ashley and I both nod and listen as he goes on speaking.

"It really is your own family who can turn on you at the end of the day. I understand and give him the benefit because I have seen him do smart deals before. Although this is out of left field and in a branch of business he's never been in before, but he told me he knows what he's doing." Nick continues.

"I'm just not sure of his new girl, but he says he loves her and that she has a business plan that she's proud of, and it will work." He says.

"Yeah, she seemed a bit opportunistic to me; I don't think they will be together that long, and he doesn't know that industry like you said." Ashley says.

The waitress then walks over, carrying three glasses and a bottle of wine on her tray.

She sets down a glass in front of each of us. And then proceeds to pour all of our glasses with the wine.

The wine looked delicious, and she left the bottle on the table for us.

"Thank you," we each say to her.

"Of course, enjoy. I'll be back to take orders." She smiles and walks off.

We each pick up our glass, say cheers, take a sip back, and are all pleased with the taste.

"Well Nick I believe in a way for you that will be solid and prosperous." I say generously.

"I think sometimes people fall hard into things when they're unsure, and possibly this girl coming along made him unsure. I don't think he's unsure about you, but with finding love and giving that a chance with all he got." I continue to say.

"Yeah, that's a good way to look at it; I know he's been seeking to find a woman. You know, ever since you left him high and dry at the altar." Nick starts to joke.

"Haha, very funny; he knew we weren't compatible." I say this while I take another sip.

"Well, we'll see. I still question the girl. I hope her intentions are good." Ashley states.

"God willing." I reply.

We all go on to pick up our menus. When Samantha comes back, we give her our orders. We enjoy more conversations of laughter and sharing memories.

Samantha brings our dishes to us and lets us know the chef hopes we enjoy them and he's glad we're here. We sit quietly, eating and savoring the yummy dishes of pasta.

Our night goes great, and we order another bottle of wine. This will be the last.

We finish out, and Nick pays the bill for us.

"I was thinking, before we go, let's check out Spence's." Ashley says this before we get up to leave.

It's not a part of the plan, and I'm not interested in going anywhere else, especially where more drinking can occur.

"Ashley, no, that's a bar, and we've already drunk through two bottles." I reply.

"It's not just that; it's more like a lounge, and I know how you feel, but just to hang out in the town a bit longer, we don't have to drink but to just look at people and enjoy the scene." She explains.

Ashley and I always joked throughout college that we were people watchers. We would sit and watch people and try to determine their lives as they passed by.

"I don't know, girl." I say to her in my tired tone.

"Please, we won't be there longer than 30 minutes. It's close by, so we don't have to go out the way anywhere and then head back home." She starts to beg.

Nick is always ready to go with Ashley, so she is just waiting for my answer.

"Okay, not longer than 30 minutes." I say.

"Yay!" Ashley shouts and does a small jump in excitement.

We leave and say our goodbyes to the staff as we exit. Our valet was ready for us, and then we headed to Spence's.

Here's to the rest of the night.

CHAPTER 8
A Look at Him

Spence's isn't that far from the Italian restaurant.

We park and walk the rest of the distance to enjoy the night breeze.

The street is vibrant, with people enjoying the Los Angeles strip. Couples walking gracefully, groups of friends walking and laughing.

"I see some of my cars parked." Nick says as he points to the black Cadillac parked in the small, designated parking area.

"You still have cars prepared? Are the drivers in there? I asked out of curiosity.

"No, I put the workers on hold till further notice. I still have contracts with parking tenants, so I'm able to leave the cars there for another week." Nick says.

His company leaves cars parked around the city in monitored areas. If a ride is requested, he sends one of his closest drivers to the location, picks up the car, and then goes to pick up the client for the ride.

"Wow, that's great, Nick." He really does have a great business going, even down to the parking arrangement, so it was easy for the driver to get the car.

"Where are the keys?" I ask as we continue to walk.

"In my truck, I have them all with me." Nick responds.

We walk further and engage in small conversation until we arrive at Spence's.

The last time I was at Spence's was for my sister, who came out to visit a month ago, before my birthday. Our sister's time was overdue, so she came for a quick visit before the family gathered for my birthday.

She wanted to go out and enjoy a night in LA while she was here visiting.

It was a pretty fun night—no heavy drinking, just some laughs and catching up with her life in Texas—and, of course, Big Sis wanted to check on me after my breakup with Marcus.

So, I felt this night could live up to that decent expectation.

At the door, we show the bouncer our identification.

As we walk in, we see a nice crowd of people socializing. There was enough room to walk through and still have your own space.

We started to look for a table. Nick sees an old friend and starts chatting with him.

"See, Sunny, this is nice; the music is good." Ashley says to me.

I looked around, and the place looked like it had been remodeled; the lights were low and of white light. There were waiters walking around, carrying drinks everywhere. Before, you had to go to the bar to get your drinks and dim-lit lighting.

People were all dressed up and sitting around laughing.

"Come on, girls, my good friend is going to take us to the rooftop part; there is more space and special seating." Nick says this and motions for us to follow.

"Yayy," Ashley says, and she grabs me in excitement.

"That's my man." She says this and walks close behind him.

We walk through the small crowd, passing people and ultimately passing by the bar.

People were all dressed, enjoying being people. This is definitely one of those places where I could sit and watch people.

That's when he catches my attention. I felt my heart race in excitement.

We got held up in our pursuit to get upstairs as some of the waiters were walking through, trying to clean up a small mess on the floor.

That's when I turn to look at him again, and this time he's looking at me.

I flush and look down.

He's very handsome. Has warm brown skin with a light caramel complexion. I noticed that he has long hair. It was brown and extremely curly. He had great, full lips, and his eyes were low but inviting. When I first saw him, it was a side view, but once we made eye contact, I was even more attracted.

He was wearing a white shirt, so it was radiating off the white light in the lounge. And from what I could see, he was wearing jeans.

He looked to be alone.

"Sorry guys, you're clear to walk through now." The waiter says after cleaning up the spilled drink,

I instantly got my attention back on track with where we were going.

But my mind keeps thinking of him.

Once we reach the top, it's a bit breezier out, but they have heaters warming up around the place. We take a seat, and our view is nice.

Nick sees another friend and starts to talk with him.

"I'll grab us drinks." Nick says.

"Wine is fine for me." I explain it to Nick.

"Okay, and babe, you want a gin and tonic?" He looks to Ashley to ask her.

"Yes, thanks, baby." She says so, and they kiss each other as he walks off with his friend to the bar.

"It's so nice and chill here tonight." I tell Ashley.

"Last time I came with April, it was packed." I explain it to her.

"Yes, I'm glad we came." She smiles, and we nod together.

The music was nice and chill; couples seemed to enjoy their evening together, and you could hear laughter throughout.

Then, my mind goes out to wander about him again. His eyes instantly came to mind.

His eyes were low but bright and welcoming.

I turn to catch myself from all these thoughts of him.

But as I look up, I see him coming up the stairs with a drink in his hands.

I can see he's stumbling a little bit.

He heads straight to the bar and starts to talk with some guys.

No judgment, but how can I be attracted to someone who is drunk and stumbling?

I see Nick say hi to him, and they engage in a small conversation.

A bit of excitement hits me; Nick may know more about him.

After a while, I see Nick walk over with our glasses.

"Here you go, ladies." Nick says it gracefully.

"Thanks baby." Ashley says it sweetly.

"Thank you, Nick," I say with a smile.

We all put up our drinks for a cheer, then took a sip back.

I want to ask Nick about the guy with eyes that keep me locked in, but I'm here to support them tonight.

So, I sit back to relax with my friends and enjoy the night.

Nick and Ashley get up soon to go and dance; they seem to be a little tipsy together.

But I guess everyone in this place is.

They don't go far, and they enjoy the rhythm and closeness of each other.

I glance around, and I don't see him anymore.

Nick brings Ashley back.

"I see some older friends; I'm going to go say hello to them. I'll be back." Nick says this as he kisses Ashley and walks away.

Ashley and I engage in some more small talk and laughter. We brought up old memories, and the time has brought me happiness. I haven't gotten through my glass of wine, but I feel good.

I keep whispering Thank You, God, to myself.

I see Nick come through the crowd to get to us.

"Nick, what's up, baby?" Ashley asks when he gets over to us.

"I feel good. I got a couple of extra shots from my friends." Nick talks in an even more tipsy manner than he did before.

He and Ashley start laughing.

Well, I guess I'll be driving us tonight.

"I'll be back," he says, then walks away again.

Wondering what is going on with him?

"I'm glad to see he's happy and looking up." Ashley says it with excitement.

I laugh with her.

"He's feeling good, alright." I say back to her.

Ashley then looks down at her phone in signal of a notification.

"Omg Nick says he's with a client that needs a ride service tonight." She explains with excitement.

And then she looked up in the direction Nick walked off in, and there he was, sitting with Nick, the man with the eyes.

He needs a ride.

God, please help him; he's Your son.

And God, please help me because I am feeling something for him.

CHAPTER 9
Take Us Home, God

I couldn't help but stare at this point; he's sitting back and can barely keep his head up. And he's sitting right across from me now.

Nick brought him over to sit at our table, and then he went off to do something else.

I noticed some of his tattoos.

The cross.

Words saying, 'God's plan, not man.'

I also see he's alone; no one has come looking for or checking on him. I see that he may be a standalone kind of guy.

And in hopes, I sense that he's kind.

But I know, on top of all that, that he's not suited to drive.

Nick isn't too far behind him on the drunken man scale.

I still have a swig of wine left in my glass.

"What's going on, Ashley? Are they okay?" I lean over to ask her.

"There is no way Nick is well enough to drive us right now." I speak anxiously.

"I believe Nick is trying to call one of his drivers to come and give him a ride home," Ashley says as she points to the man with the eyes.

"Okay, hopefully they find him someone." I say to her.

She gets up and leaves.

I'm instantly more awake than I was before. The crowd all look more intoxicated than they were just seconds ago.

The room seemed to quiet down, and everyone looked like they were trying to find their way.

It is time to go.

I look at him again, sitting across from me, and this time I notice him looking at me. His eyes are low, and his demeanor tells it all: he is drunk.

Ashley comes back over to us, sitting at the table.

"Hey, what's going on now? Where is Nick?" I ask her eagerly.

This guy is drunk; I'm ready to go, and the night is getting late.

"He's having trouble finding a driver for Omega." Ashley tells me.

"Who is Omega?" I immediately asked her.

"Him," Ashley says as she points at him, sitting right across from me. The same man that made my heart flutter when my attention was caught by him. The same man who made eye contact with me that was so intense that it felt like he already knew me. The same man that is drunk right now.

"Him…this is Omega?" I ask. I felt a bit of excitement at finally knowing his name.

"Hey, yeah." Omega manages to mumble. Kind of slumped over.

I sit quietly.

Ashley goes back to check her phone.

"I'll be back." She says this and walks away again.

I try to speak to her, but she's gone before I can get a word in.

Omega is still sitting there and looks to be going to sleep.

I thought I would ask him if he needed water, but I saw no sign of waiters.

Then I see Ashley walking back over to us.

"So, there's a bit of a dilemma." She states it in a worried manner.

"Okay?" I say this in question.

"Nick is having a hard time corresponding, let alone getting a driver. He doesn't have anyone in close proximity to pick up Omega. And he himself can't drive, period. So, I continued to look all through his driver's app, and we had no luck. But Omega requested a ride." Ashley says.

"Wow, that's too bad." I say to her. I feel sorry for Omega.

"So, I thought maybe you could drive him home." Ashley blurts it out quickly.

There is no way she is serious.

I know she can tell by the look on my face that I wasn't feeling her request.

"Please, Sunday, it would mean so much to Nick." Ashley starts begging.

I start shaking my head.

"No, girl, I can't do that." I say to her.

I want to be of help, but I'm not doing that much.

"Please, Sunday, all the information is on the phone." She hands over the phone.

"His address, and see, it's not even 25 minutes away." She points it out on the phone.

"Girl, I can't do this; I don't even know this man." I said to her as I began to stand up from my seat.

"Omega is nice; he's the one investor and food junkie that Nick was talking about at dinner earlier." Ashley continues to say.

"I don't care about that, Ashley; I came with you and Nick, and I planned on leaving that way." I say right back to her.

Although I don't want him drunk here, I can't be the one to take him.

"Why can't you ask anyone else? Any of those guys Nick was talking to all night?" I quickly asked her.

"They're pretty drunk too." She responds.

This is the exact thing that I don't like about going out and being the only mindful, sober one.

"How did he even get here himself?" I ask her.

"Most likely, he came with someone, and they left him." She says to me.

Wow, that's low.

"Look, Sunday, I know we could call Uber or another driving service, but this would be so beneficial to Nick's company. Omega would tip well; leave a great review, and he knows great people that would help with Nick's investment because we helped him tonight." She explained it to me.

"That's all so nice, but you can't do it? Or at least come with me?" I say.

"I have to take Nick home, plus it wouldn't look good for the owner of the company to be drunk in the car with the client." She explained it to me.

"How was Nick going to manage to get us home anyway if he was going to drink like that?" I ask her sternly.

"I think he got a little, hopeful, or a little too ahead of himself when finding out that he could be back in business tonight," Ashley says.

I stand and think about everything.

Tonight, I want to be of help to my friends who have been working so hard to run this business, and I do want Omega to be okay.

I look over, and I see him straightening himself up now. He looks so tired.

God, I'm Your servant; what must I do?

I felt a nudge in my spirit. I felt the provision of God, and mostly, I felt it in my heart to help.

"Okay, fine, I'll take him." I finally say to Ashley.

"Really, yes, yes, yes. Thank you so much, Sunday. You have no idea how much this means to us and what this will do for us." She says this while jumping with excitement.

"You are such a gift from God for all of us, even Omega." She continues.

"I'll get the keys, and one of the cars for the ride service is parked not too far, the valet will pull it up." She says, then hurries off.

I turn to look at Omega, and he's looking at me.

I adore his eyes and feel that he's a respectable guy.

God willing, please be with us tonight.

CHAPTER 10
God is in his Heart

The valet has the car parked right outside Spence's.

Ashley and I walk side by side as Omega and Nick follow behind us.

I'm trying to make this quick so I can get this man home.

"Thanks again, girl. Here's the phone with the location to his house and all other information on him." She says this as she hands me the phone.

I know the look on my face says it all, and I'm so over this night.

Nick and Omega are holding on to each other as Nick tries to open the passenger side door to the black Suburban SUV for Omega.

They are so drunk barely holding on.

"Let me know if you need anything at all. I have my phone on me, and I'm going straight home with Nick." Ashley says.

She opened the driver's side door for me and gave me a big hug.

"I thank God and you for all of this." She says as she walks off.

I get into the car, and the interior is all blacked out and beautiful. The dash panel and the screen are all colorful, with plenty buttons for the gadgets.

But I have no interest in discovering how to use any of that right now; I just want to get this man home.

I look over, and his head is laid back, eyes closed.

I hope he just sleeps the whole way.

I see on the phone that the directions say 27 minutes until arrival. He looks to be staying in the high-end suburbs of the city.

I notice he isn't wearing his seat belt.

"Hey Omega, I'm ready to go. But you don't have your seatbelt on yet. Can you put it on?" I ask him.

He doesn't move for a minute.

"Sure thing. I'm glad you're finally talking to me." He says to me.

He motions to put his seatbelt on, then turns to smile at me before laying his head back.

I wonder what he meant by that. I'm not going to ask him, though.

I press the start engine button, then head straight to the destination.

The night air has gotten cooler, but I keep the windows down a bit to give Omega some air as he sits there with his head back, leaning on the headrest.

I also needed the air, as I was thinking of how fine Omega is.

I can't believe that the very first man that caught my interest tonight, in a while at that, is the very man I was taking home because he's too drunk to get himself there.

I don't even know what to say to him.

I figured to just let him sleep.

But that thought still crossed my mind of what he meant when he said, "Sure thing. I'm glad you're finally talking to me."

I hear him start to groan. I instantly think that he may need to throw up.

"Are you okay?" Do you need more air? There are a couple of water bottles in the back seat." I tell him.

"I'm ight, you just smell really good." Omega says to me.

I didn't expect that.

"Thank you." That is all I can manage to say back.

"You smell like a human bouquet." He manages to say.

"Like freshly picked roses and flowers and shit." He says.

"My bad excuse my language." He continues to say with a little giggle.

"Thank you." I say again.

I'm kind of thrown off by his compliments.

I keep focusing on the drive and looking head-on.

"How are you feeling?" I ask him.

"I'm floating because the most beautiful girl in the world is here with me." He says this as he starts giggling, like a kid around his crush.

Again, I'm lost for words.

I just proceeded to the destination to get him home.

I see his head moving back and forth as he manages to sleep.

He then grabs his beanie from his head, and it falls to the floor.

"How are you feeling, Omega? We are almost home." I say to him.

I look over, and he has a small smile on his face.

"This is great." I hear him mumble as he rests his head again.

I have no idea what he means by that. I have no idea how to have a conversation with him.

I just want to get him home and hope he doesn't throw up on the way.

I say a small prayer in my head. I pray that God gives Omega some strength to keep to himself till he gets into his room and then falls asleep.

I look over to him again, but this time in admiration.

He really is handsome. I can't look for too long; I must keep my eyes on the road.

But I have a mental image in my head, and I'm pleased with his company. Although he's intoxicated, his presence feels like what I need.

All his drunken words have been nice. Nothing is disrespectful or uncomfortable.

The GPS signals tell me to turn right up ahead, bringing me back into reality.

I see that it says 10 minutes until I reach his destination.

I feel sadness come over me from knowing I will be releasing Omega soon and not knowing when I will see him again.

I don't go out often, and after what Nick and Ashley pulled tonight, I can't rely on them to say we will have an easy night, no heavy drinking, and then go home.

But I take the change in direction as an opportunity to help someone and be near a man; I feel attracted to.

Give God the glory and move on.

I see his head still rocking in the passenger seat.

Poor guy, but now we are looking at 5 minutes till I get him home.

"Hey Omega, we aren't too far now." I tell him.

"Okay beautiful." He manages to respond to me.

A blush comes over my face. This time, my cheeks feel red hot, my heart runs as if in a race, and my butterfly starts to open up from the cocoon.

I must get ready to say goodbye.

I pull up to Omega's home. It's a nice two-story building with long modern windows, all white-beige color, and a huge cherry blossom tree planted outside.

It's the only cherry blossom tree I see in his neighborhood.

His pathway to the door is lit up with white lights.

From what I can see in the darkness, it's a beautiful home.

"We're here." I say to him as I put the car in park.

He looks up at me and gives me a gentle smile, and it pulls me; my heart races, and I feel my muscles weaken.

I have never felt so fluttered by someone, especially someone in this manner.

But this man has my interest.

I give him a gentle smile back.

Then, a long stare happens. I was the first to look away.

"Have a goodnight." I managed to say it to him.

He opens the door slowly, using the little strength he has.

I was considering getting out to help him, but physical contact may be too much right now.

I know my strengths and weaknesses. Right now, I need to call on God to handle both.

Plus, I see that he's managing to do it.

"Thank you; this meant a lot. I hope you make it home safely." He says, standing outside the door on the passenger side.

"You are a beautiful lady, okay?" He says it with a smile.

Again, I feel that pulling on the inside. I feel like a young girl in high school or something.

"Thank you, and God bless." I gracefully reply.

"Thank you, and God bless you too." He says this as he closes the door.

My whole body shook not at the closing of the door but at his response.

He has God in his heart.

I pull off as I see him get inside his home.

Ashley had sent a text while I was driving Omega home, asking if I was okay and to keep the car at my apartment until tomorrow.

I quickly texted her, Yes, I'm good, and okay, I'll keep the car.

I go on to drive home. Thinking of him. More than I have thought of anyone before, let alone a man, especially after freeing myself from Marcus.

What are your plans, God?

CHAPTER 11
Garden Ministries

I made it home safely and immediately, thanked God.

I go to my room, take my shoes off, take my dress off, and then shower.

It's about 1:45 a.m. I've been up this late on a night before church once before, but not from being out all night at a lounge.

I usually lead the Bible study every other Sunday, and it's my Sunday.

Thankfully, I have my notes prepared and ready to talk about King David.

I get into bed and realize my mind is still active. Actively thinking about Omega.

Maybe I should have invited him to church, but I was so caught up in the feeling I was experiencing with him.

Everything happened so fast.

Plus, I figured there was no way he could get out of bed and get to church after the late night or early morning he just had.

And then again, I should never assume.

I grab my phone and see that it's 2:30 a.m. now. I put on my calming sleep noises from my Spotify app, clear my mind, and let my eyes get heavy until I fall asleep.

I'm woken up at 6:15 a.m. by my alarm.

Since it's my day to lead the Bible study, I get up early to be there at 8:45 a.m., as Bible study starts at 9 a.m.

I need to have my morning prayer, make coffee, and have breakfast.

I also need to call Ashley to see if she's going to make it to church.

I get on my knees in my designated prayer area and my room's study area. I have a small lounge couch, my desks, a prayer mat, my journals, books, and devotionals. I always keep a fresh bouquet of flowers in this area. That is also where I have my notes for my study of King David.

He is one of my favorite characters from the good book. I know his story so well and find new revelations in it every time I teach it. I have prepared my scriptures and know what direction I would like to go in.

I pray: *Heavenly Father, Lord of Lords, King of Kings, my Savior. Thank You for waking me up this morning and for giving me Your breath of life to prosper through another day, completing Your will for Your Kingdom. I thank You for watching over me as I was sleeping at night. I thank You for all You are doing, and for what I do and do not see. I trust in You, and all I have is at Your feet. Please have the Holy Spirit work through me as I lead Bible study today. Please help me to be a blessing to a lost sheep today; use me in any way You desire, Lord. I am Yours. Thank You. You are beautiful. Amen.*

I arise from my prayer position and feel the peace of God come over me.

I smile and look up.

I grab my phone and head to the kitchen to prepare myself breakfast.

I call Ashley as I take my eggs out of the fridge to make an omelet and a bagel out of the pantry to toast.

"Hey Sunday." Ashley answers with a groan.

Yeah, she's hungover.

"How are you, my friend?" I ask as I chop up the ingredients for my omelet.

"Well..." she took a moment to answer.

"I'm feeling like I was hit by a truck, then my shirt caught onto the back hook and it dragged me for about 3 miles." She explained it to me.

"Wow girl." I say to her. She is one for dramatic descriptions.

"Yeah, when Nick and I got home, we drank some more in celebration of you helping us get the company going." She says.

I think back to Omega and wonder how he's feeling today.

"Well Ash I'm happy to have helped, but I'm sorry you're feeling hungover. How's Nick?" I ask her.

"He's passed out still, but I see his work phone going off with business notifications. I'm telling you all we needed was one client that would pay out, alert the revenue, and then investors would come back in," she says.

"You and Omega did that for us, but especially for Nick." She says this, and I hear gratitude in her voice.

"Thank you; you truly are a great friend, and sorry again for putting you out there." She says.

"Well, I'm happy to help. I love you both. And that's why I went out with you guys' last night to help; I just didn't think it would be that kind of help." I respond.

"But Omega was simple, and everything went well." I continue to say.

"Good, I'm glad. I felt that it would be a simple arrangement between the two of you." She says.

My heart leaps a bit. Part of me had no interest in being involved with a drunk, but another part of me was happy it happened.

I liked the interaction I had with him.

"Yeah, it was good." I simply respond. I can't run these feelings over and over.

"Are you able to come to church with me? It's my week to lead Bible study." I ask her to try to change the subject.

"I don't think so, girl. I won't make it through. Please just pray for us." Ashley says.

"But you can take the company car. Nick was saying he was going to pay you for the service and that you could use the car today for anything you needed. If you need more gas, I'll cash app you." She says.

I'm almost done making my omelet, and my bagel is in the toaster.

"Okay, that would be nice. Thank you." I respond.

"I didn't get a chance to check out all the tech stuff in the car last night. And whatever he gives me can be sent as a donation for the church." I continue to say.

"Sounds good. I love you, girl. Call me afterwards to tell me how the study went." She says to me.

"Okay, I'm going over King David." I say to her.

"I know you love that man, girl." She says it with a playful giggle.

She always teased me about how I would be with him if King David were around today.

"Bye girl, I love you." I say, then hang up the phone.

She's a good and honest friend. I know she would go to church if she wasn't feeling hungover.

I sat my breakfast plate down at the table, grabbed my Keurig coffee, and began praying and eating.

I think about my notes and the story of King David and his Psalms, which I'm going over this morning.

Then, my mind starts to think of Omega. He was handsome and kind. He seemed to be doing well for himself, given his occupation and how nice his home looked.

He seemed so sincere and grateful to hear the words' God bless' and then says it in return.

Who really was that man?

I finish my breakfast, feeling satisfied and full.

I go to my closet to get my clothes ready for church.

I picked out a casual outfit. My purple summer dress. It is long, and at the bottom trim, it is lined with flowers.

It's comfortable and classy.

I get my sparkle-studded sandal heels for my feet.

I go to my bathroom and apply a light layer of makeup.

I got my curls moisturized and then put on a pair of purple earrings and a few bracelets to match.

I feel ready for the Lord. I gather my notes for the Bible study off my desk and read over today's verses. I'm reading Psalm 139.

I checked the clock. It's almost 8:15 a.m., and it takes me about 25 minutes to get there.

I have been attending 'His Sow Baptist Church' for almost seven years. I came here first by myself, looking for a new church home after moving out of my parents' home.

My sister April finally came after a couple of attempts, and still comes when she's in town visiting me.

Since being there, I have started Garden Ministries with a few other church members, including Ashley. It's all about encouraging new growth and constant faith in God. And even when we are low and feel stuck, it's because we are buried as His seeds, which eventually blossom up into beautiful plants and vegetables. We get pruned in the process for His glory and His love. We teach the right essentials of God for the growing process, such as being watered and fed by God's word and then pruned by Him.

Our mission statement for Garden Ministries: Come all who are seeking something far greater than what this world can offer. Something that has all the power. Something that was designed for you specifically and purposefully to give Him the glory. He's the God of Gods. Lord of the Lords. King of Kings. All it takes is faith the size of a mustard seed to be planted so He can grow you, water you, prune you, feed you, establish you, and watch how you become a fruitful garden. He already paid the ultimate sacrifice; now you must give Him your seed so He can make it new. So, He can make a garden out of you.

And I'm so thankful to Pastor Millstone for supporting us, too.

We have reached a lot of young members, even some children in the community.

I was hoping to spread more about it at the school where I applied to teach.

But the active members we do have are supportive, and that makes all the difference.

I grab my Bible, notepad, phone, purse, and keys to Nick's company car.

I really enjoyed driving luxury, although I'm grateful for my sports Honda. I feel blessed because it's in good running condition and in great shape, which is a luxury in itself. Thank you, Jesus.

I lock up my home and head to the parking garage. I hopped right in and began to adjust the radio/Bluetooth and all the other technology gadgets I didn't get to try last night.

I was solely focused on getting Omega home.

And then focused on how fine he was.

A rush of excitement comes over me as I think of him.

Then my eyes look over slightly, and my attention is caught by something on the passenger side floor.

A beanie, it's Omega's beanie.

I remember him pulling it off his head while in and out of his sleepy daze; I just didn't notice he hadn't grabbed it when I dropped him off.

I reach to pick it up.

And I see some writing in Japanese.

He hasn't reached out for it to be returned. He could possibly still be sleeping.

A thought came over me: I'll return it to him after church.

"Thank You, Holy Spirit, for a generous thought." I say it aloud.

I put the beanie in the glove compartment and pulled out of the garage, heading to church.

I catch myself overly smiling, and I know it's because I'll possibly be seeing Omega again.

CHAPTER 12
Walking in Peace

Today, during Bible study, we were blessed with two new guests who were looking to join the church.

Everyone loves a good King David lesson.

His victorious and very relatable story is a huge light in the coming to Jesus.

And everyone spoke, which ultimately made the Bible study more active.

The members grabbed some of the coffee and donuts before heading into the sanctuary to hear Pastor Millstone preach God's word.

And the word was from Jeremiah 29:11, speaking of God's plan.

Learning to sit down and submit to God's will.

Because His plans are far greater and will give Him all the glory.

The congregation shouted and cheered in agreement.

And we were blessed with another sermon and prayer for God's children.

Members often gather and talk to one another at the end of service. I remember I must give Omega back his beanie.

So, I quickly say hello and goodbye to my church sisters and brothers and, of course, Pastor Millstone before heading to the car.

I look in the compartment where I put Nick's work phone, which has Omega's address, and I pull it up.

30 minutes from church.

I pull out my phone to call Ashley and let her know.

"Hey Sunday, how was Bible study and service?" Ashley asks.

"It was great, speaking on God's plan of hope and future for His children." I respond.

"That's good." She says.

I think for a short while about how I'm going to tell her about going to Omega's house.

"So, I noticed Omega left his beanie in the car, and I was going to his home to return it to him." I finally say.

The line is silent for a while.

"Sunday girl…..what?" She says it in an amusing tone.

"What made you want to do that?" she goes on asking.

"Nick can easily return it to him." She says.

"Unless you're trying to see him again?" Ashley says it in a quirky tone.

"I don't mind being helpful." I mildly respond.

"No, girl, I feel this; you must like him. What happened between you too last night?" she asks.

"Nothing; he could barely keep his head up. He was nice and all, and I want to return the favor by giving him back his beanie." I say it to her easily.

I can't have her break me down.

"Sure thing, he was nice." Ashley says it mockingly.

"You like him, and I'm positive he likes you too," Ashley says.

I flutter a bit at the thought of it.

"You know, this is what I mean by playing in the field; you opened up, and now you like someone you least likely expected," she goes on saying.

"I didn't say I liked him; I just wanted him to have his beanie back. Stop jumping everywhere with this. I just wanted you to know where I'm headed." I respond.

"Okay, then, and just to let you know, Nick is going to have great things to say about him as well. He's a successful guy. I know he's single and has a very interesting life." She goes on to say.

My interest continues to peak.

"Thanks for all the heads up; okay, I'm going to go now." I quickly say to her.

"Okay, then, girl, call me afterwards." Ashley says.

"Sure will, bye," I say right before hanging up.

I can't let her throw me off from what is going to be a simple task.

I grab Nick's work phone and scroll through to find Omega's number.

Not letting nerves run through me, I hit the call button.

It rang until it reached the automated voicemail.

I'm not going to let it stop me; I assume he's still sleeping.

I head in the direction of the GPS and play my Christian R&B playlist for the ride.

When I pull up, I notice again just how beautiful the house is, but now with a daytime view.

I parked right where I had parked last night, and I noticed the front door opening, and I saw that it was him coming out.

I feel my temperature rising. I must keep my frame strong.

"God, give me strength." I say to myself as I open the door to get out of the car.

He walks down the driveway, getting closer and closer to me.

He's wearing grey sweat shorts and a white T-shirt.

His long, beautiful, curly hair hangs down, and I love how it's a bit messy.

"Whoa, hey, what's up, beautiful lady?" He shouts with a smile on his face.

He is more awake and active than he was last night, brighter, and as sweet as ever.

I'm even more entwined than before; this man has my attention.

But I'm going to remain within myself and keep my composure.

"You're back; God is good and really real," he says.

"I never thought I was going to see you again." He continues.

We are now face-to-face.

"Hey, yes, it's good to see you and that you're doing much better." I respond peacefully.

I try to keep a small smile.

"Was that you that just called me? I thought it was Nick calling to chew me out about last night, but then he was over it when I called my business partners about Drive Nick." He says.

Those two think everything is funny.

"Yes, I wanted to call and tell you that you left your beanie in the car and that I would return it to you." I responded to him.

"Thank you; I really appreciate it. And I can't stop saying how beautiful you look. I like your dress. Are you coming from church or something?" He goes on to ask.

"Thank you, Omega, and yes, I just left service, and I noticed your beanie on my way to church this morning." I say to him.

I go back to the car to grab the beanie.

My heart is still racing. I can feel him watching me.

I take the beanie and hand it to him.

"Yes, my beanie from Tokyo. Thank you; this means a lot. One of my favorite beanies. And one of the best trips I've taken." He explains.

Wow, he's a traveler.

"That's cool; how was Tokyo?" I ask him.

"Simply put, it's a great place to be a tourist who loves to eat food, especially ramen." He says it with a smile.

"Yes, ramen is great." I say it in an excited tone.

I haven't had ramen in so long.

"What does it say on the front?" I asked, pointing to the writing in Japanese.

"It says 'walking in peace'." He says this, looking down at the writing.

"I love that." I compliment.

"Sorry for last night, by the way; I feel that I messed up having a chance to really talk to you by being so drunk." He tells me.

"I've been letting go of some things in my life; drinking hard is one of them. I asked for a sign from God that if I could see something beautiful, I'd let the drink go. I know God doesn't work like that, but then again, he does because I saw you; I was already pretty wasted though." He explains.

I looked down with the biggest smile on my face.

"Thank you, Omega; you're sweet. I was happy to help get you home and to help Nick with his car business." I tell him.

"Ya, he's been a cool friend, and that was our first time seeing each other in a cool minute. I was glad I could use his car service and not worry about anyone else taking me." Omega says.

"Ya, he kept saying, we saved the business for him; your ride request and me being able to be the driver gave him the one revenue for your partners to bring him investors." I explain it to him.

"Yeah, I know, he was telling me all about it when we spoke this morning. I didn't even know that was what he was up against." He says.

"We were out last night because he lost his main investor, who was his cousin, and it threatened him to lose the business. His girlfriend is my best friend, and she asked me to join them for a night out to lift his spirits." I tell him.

"And we ended up at Spence's to hang out a little more. That's when I saw you." I say.

"It all worked out; Nick is still home, passed out with a hangover from everything." I tell him.

We both laugh.

"That's great to hear. I still wish I was coherent, but ya I think it all worked out." He says.

"This whole experience has made me look in the mirror to start making changes within myself." He continues.

He stops his words for a second.

"I wish I had gotten your name before it all happened." He goes on to say.

That's right, I never gave him my name.

"I'm Sunday." I swiftly told him.

"Wow, meeting Sunday on a Sunday, I like it. I already feel the change," he says.

I smile at him shyly because I feel the change, too.

"Well, Sunday, can I have your number?" He kindly asks.

"Yes, I'd like that." I tell him.

He grabs his phone out of his pocket and hands it to me. I enter it and hand it back to him.

"I should probably get going now." I tell him

"Yeah, I'll call you in a little bit when you get settled in at home. If that's okay?" He asks me.

"Yes, that's good." I respond.

There was a moment there when we were both looking to hug one another, but we resisted.

It's way too soon to make any contact.

"Alright then, let me get the door for you." He says, walking ahead of me to open the car door.

"Thank you." I tell him as I get into the truck.

"Bye Sunday; see you later." He says

"Bye now." I reply as he closes the door.

I start the engine and take off.

"Wow God, he is kind. I hope I can get to know him more and see You in him." I speak to God.

"Your will, God." I say it loudly.

I grab my phone and see there are a whole bunch of texts from Ashley asking if I'm okay and what's going on.

I call her.

She immediately answers.

"Hello, that took you forever. I was worried." She says this, shouting at me.

"It wasn't that long, and everything is fine." I tell her.

"Okay, so what happened?" She goes on to ask.

"Well, we briefly talked, and he apologized that we couldn't have a better conversation last night because he was drunk. And then he asked for my number." I explain it to her.

"What, omg, yes, yes, yes!!" She shouts.

"Did you give it to him?" Ashley asked me.

"Yes." I simply reply.

"Yayyy, get it, best friend." She exclaims.

"Ashley, whatever, it's just to talk." I told her back.

"I know you, girl, and I know you're not easily moved by men to give them your number. I knew you were feeling him." She says.

"I think he's nice. He was nice last night and nice today, while he's clear and sober. Just nice." I explain it to her.

"Ya, and fine, girl." She shouts with humor.

"Wow, this is so great," Ashley says excitedly.

"Yes, okay, I'm going to get food and make it home. I'll call you soon." I say to her.

"Okay, then, my graceful friend, I love you, girl. Call me later. You know I want more details of what y'all talk about." She says.

"Alright then, bye, girl; I love you too." I reply.

The phone call ends.

And I'm full of smiles.

CHAPTER 13
Can I Pick the Place?

Once home, I'm ready to eat my Wing Stop order. Lemon pepper and original hot wings with a side of fries.

I go to my room and put on my comfortable loungewear of shorts and a T-shirt.

I sit in front of the TV and decide to watch Family Feud.

I pray over my food, *Heavenly Father. I thank You for a beautiful day filled with beautiful worship and Sunday service. Thank You for providing me with this food that will nourish my body. I love You. Amen.*

I dig right in; everything is delicious, and Family Feud is hilarious.

Sitting back and full, I notice the time is almost 4 p.m.; around this time, my mom calls to check in. She asks the same questions about work, ministry plans, and if I'm dating. Then we'll usually do a 4-way with grandma for her input and the for April to tell us any wedding plans she is putting together.

My phone begins to ring as expected.

I grab it and quickly answer while laughing at a funny remark made by Steve Harvey.

"Hey, ma."

"Umm, hey to you too, ma." It's a man's deep voice.

I look at my phone and see a number I don't recognize on the screen.

"Oh, I'm sorry. I thought this was my mom calling." I reply embarrassingly.

I hear laughter.

I couldn't help but laugh too.

Could this be him?

"This is Omega." He responds.

Yes, it's him.

"Hi Omega, how are you?" I ask him.

I sit back and settle myself on the couch.

He called, and I'm excited to talk with him.

"I'm doing pretty well. Were you waiting for your Mom to call?" He asks me.

"Umm, yes, she usually calls right around this time on Sundays." I replied to him.

"Oh, ok, I don't want to hold up the line for Mom's call." He says.

"No, it's ok; she would have called by now; it's possible she's at an after-church event." I tell him.

"How was service?" He asks me.

"It was great; Pastor Millstone spoke on God's plan in Jeremiah 29:11, and I led the Bible study for my group this morning." I tell him.

My heart starts melting at his interest in church.

"What church do you go to?" He asked.

"His Sow Baptist Church." I tell him.

"I've heard of it. I would like to go with you sometime." He says.

"That would be great; Pastor Millstone is always happy for new members." I tell him.

"I believe my parents went there many years ago; they stopped going when life got hectic, draining them. My dad felt bad about the times he would fall asleep during the service." He says.

We both laugh.

"That's cool your parents attended; people always say it feels like family there." I tell him.

It's true the church is very open, and Pastor Millstone just wants to see an effort. He believes that the word will resonate no matter what. And most importantly, the church is held to the truth, and Pastor Millstone encourages members to read their Bibles daily.

"I'm looking forward to it." He says.

"Where are your parents living now?" I ask him.

"They're here in California, debating moving back to Texas. They love the country. They have a home there and have been living back and forth for years." He says.

"My sister lives in Texas with her man," I tell him.

"Oh, cool, have you been?" He asks.

"Not yet," I tell him.

"Do you have siblings?" I ask him.

"Yeah, my little brother passed almost a month ago." He speaks lowly.

"I'm so sorry." I reply.

I shift in my seat. I didn't expect to hear that.

"Yeah, he was hit by a car. My family and I have been dealing with it." He says

I hear his tone getting lower. It is obviously still hard to talk about.

"Jesus is the only real comfort for that type of loss," I tell him.

"I know, I've just been trying to get out of my own way to see that." He says.

I feel his honesty and brokenness.

"Can I say a prayer for you?" I ask him.

"Yeah please." He responds.

"Heavenly Father, our refuge, our comforter. Please lead Omega's life so He can see Your hands on things. The hardest part of life is death, but You overcame that on the cross. Remind Omega of that victory so he knows You are real, King of all things, and are here to bring him all that he needs. Let him come to You for everything. And I thank You for this moment to bring us together. May Your peace fall upon us. Amen." I say.

"Amen," he says.

'That was great; it meant a lot." He says.

"I would really like to see you and have lunch or dinner with you." He says.

"Ok, I would like that too." I tell him.

An honest lunch or dinner will be good, and I love that we can pray together.

I'm excited and hopeful. Thank You, God.

"I'm looking forward to seeing you again and talking more with you in person." He says.

Wow, he's so kind.

"So am I." I tell him.

"What's your schedule like? I would like to take you to dinner tonight." He says.

Wow, tonight. I'm not sure if that's too soon.

But then again, I'm the one who felt led to just take his beanie to him without hesitation.

We can't deny the attraction.

Holy Spirit, what should I say?

"Ok, let's do dinner tonight." I replied to him.

"Alright, do you mind if I pick the place? And I can pick you up around 8 p.m.?" Omega asks.

"Ok." I softly reply.

"Ok, cool. I'll call when I'm on the way. I'll just need your address." He says.

"I'll text it to you." I say.

"Cool." He replies.

"Ok, see you soon." He says.

"Alright. Bye." I say this before hanging up.

I'm going out with him.

I have to get ready. I have to call Ashley. I have to pray.

CHAPTER 14
New Plans

I get on my knees and start praying to God: Hello, Heavenly Father. I want to say thank You for a beautiful day so far. Service was good, Bible study went well, and I met a man who knows You. And I know You saw that we have a dinner date tonight. I believe he is in my life in Your will, and I will maintain the calling You have for me. Please protect and be the sole guide for the evening. Amen.

When it comes to praying for a man, I have learned from experience that praying for a man to be with me instead of on one accord with God and me doesn't work.

Being on one accord will give us a safe place within each other's presence to open and have honest communication, so we can really get to know each other and what this could become.

I must let God be the miracle behind bringing His children together for love.

And I only started to pray when things were going bad, causing damage.

Pray must be a 24/7 thing.

Marcus was all I wanted, and I made changes to my values because I didn't want to lose him; I felt that I needed him.

When things started going wrong, and I was risking my walk with God, I started to pray. It's never too late to pray, but the damage has already been done.

God wanted me to know that I only needed Him.

And the whole mess of a soul-tie with Marcus was to teach me that.

And God's grace was still on me, and I'm redeemed, and my relationship with God is stronger than ever.

Omega is already a different guy from Marcus or any other at that.

Marcus never brought up God first, let alone wanted to pray.

And it's not to compare, but this new experience is already showing what happens when I wait on God.

And so, I'm putting it all in God's hands and will be praying every step of the way.

I get up from praying, thank God, and grab my phone to call Ashley.

I need her to know about my whereabouts just in case something goes wrong.

Ashley shared her whereabouts with Nick up until three months after they started dating.

"Hey Sunny." She says when she answers.

"Hey girl, how are you feeling? Still hungover?" I ask her.

"We feel better after eating. How are you? Have you talked to Omega yet?" She asks me in a curious tone.

I roll my eyes at her playfulness.

"Yes, I just got off the phone with him. He asked me out to dinner tonight. And I told him yes." I say with excitement.

I hear her make a yelp of excitement.

"My girl got a date with Omega." She shouts.

"Hey, babe, guess what??" She yells at Nick.

"What?" I hear him respond in the background.

"Omega and Sunday are going out tonight." She shouts.

"What! That's great!" I hear him say.

I exhaled in relief at his response.

Nick knows him the most and wouldn't have me date a jerk.

His cousin was the exception because everyone always hypes their family members up.

I hear Nick grab the phone.

"Hey Sunday, yeah, Omega is a cool guy. He has his own business; I'll let him tell you about it. He's one of those drama-free guys who keeps to himself and loves food. Kind of your average guy, but with his own twist on things. And he believes in God." Nick says to me.

"I like those qualities, and he mentioned some of those things to me while we were on the phone." I tell Nick.

"Ya, I know he's going to amp all of that up for you tonight." He says.

"Really, what do you mean?" I ask, kind of shyly.

"He doesn't just date around. I've heard him say that he's looking for a wife, not just girlfriends." He says.

"So, he never asks a woman out unless there is a real interest there." He goes on to tell me.

My being melts at the thought of him.

But I'm still leaving it in God's hands.

"Wow, that's great to know. So, it should be a good time." I reply.

"Ya have fun Sunday." Nick says, then I hear him pass the phone back to Ashley.

"Yes, something so special and different is happening with all of this; I can feel it, Sunny. You deserve to have a good time and for him to spoil you with compliments about how beautiful you are and to feed you some good food." Ashley says.

"I just knew it was a good thing to ask you to take him home last night. Nick has two meetings tomorrow for investors. His drivers are ready to start working, and you got a date with a good guy." Ashley continues.

And I agree; it all turned out to be good. Thank God.

Even with all Omega has to deal with, such as the loss of his little brother, it feels that we can both bring sweet peace to each other's lives.

"Thanks, Ashley, and tell Nick thank you as well. I'm excited." I tell her.

"What about the car?" I ask her.

"I got the key to your place; if we need the car we'll come grab the keys; just leave on the kitchen countertop." She says.

"And is he picking you up?" She continues to ask me.

"Yes, he said he'd be here at 8 p.m." I tell her.

"Ok, I still need your whereabouts, even though we know and trust him." She responds.

"Of course, I'll let you know all the details once I know. He said he wanted to pick the place and all." I tell her.

"Ya sounds like him; Nick says he's the food guy, so he'll for sure be taking you out to get some good food and probably someplace new. He has a lot of food connections." Ashley says.

"Ya, he was telling me how he went to Tokyo for ramen." I tell her.

"Yep, that's Omega." She says, laughing.

"Have fun! What are you going to wear?" She goes on to ask me.

"I'm not sure yet; I'm going to go pick something out now." I respond.

"I know you'll be beautiful. Ok, remember to let me know your whereabouts and all the juicy details." She says.

"And if you need anything, let me know." She says.

"I will, girl. Thanks so much. I love you. Bye." I say this before hanging up.

"I love you too, bye." She says, then hangs up.

I feel like I'm floating. I'm so excited.

I text Omega my address and the directions on how to get to my floor.

Now, I need to figure out what to wear.

I'm thinking of a dress as I head to my room closet.

My phone notified me that a text message had come in.

"Got it; see you soon." Omega says.

"Ok, see ya." I respond back.

I look in the mirror and see the big smile on my face.

It feels great to smile and be excited about something new, but I also want to take my time and not get ahead of myself.

I go to look for the white dress I had in mind, and I get out a couple of pieces of jewelry to match it.

I start to get ready with a natural makeup look and my natural curls, which gracefully bounce with every move.

Time is moving so fast.

I get a text from him letting me know he'll be here in 20 minutes.

I finish the last touches to my look; I smile in approval.

My long white fitted dress looks great on me.

I take a deep breath.

"Thank You, God, for this opportunity; please don't leave me, Holy Spirit."

I hear a knock on my door.

I gracefully walked over to the front door.

I open it to see his handsome, welcoming face.

And he's holding a beautiful, huge bouquet of red and pink roses.

We're in awe looking at each other, and the moment felt like it lasted forever.

CHAPTER 15
Something Sweet

"Hey, wow, you look so beautiful." He says this while giving me a passionate look.

Thos eyes of his keep me locked in.

He puts his head down bashfully.

"Thank you, Omega; you look handsome." I tell him.

He is dressed nicely in a blue shirt with the Louis Vuitton logo.

He has suede blue shoes to match the color of his shirt and a pair of dark blue slacks.

This must be his color, and must I say it looks good on him.

His long, curly hair is tied up back in a ponytail.

And his smile is bigger than ever.

The look we give each other is honest and intense.

And I see him come near me for a hug; this is the time we finally come into contact.

I grab the roses and quickly put them in a vase with water.

"This is going to be a good night; are you ready to go? We'll eat some good food and hang out." He asks.

"Yes," I tell him as I turn to lock my door.

We smile and continue to look at each other as we walk near the elevator.

We hit the bottom floor that leads to the street, and he leads the way to his Mercedes car parked in the guest parking.

It's a beautiful all-white Mercedes Benz.

I try not to lavish on material things, but I have always wanted a Mercedes truck.

"Your car is amazing," I tell him as he opens the passenger-side door for me.

"Thank you; she's a good car and fun to drive." He replies.

"I usually drive my Bronco truck, but I wanted to bring out the amazing car for the beautiful lady." He says this once he's inside the car.

The dashboard is all lit up with multiple colors. It looks like a spaceship full of touch-screen technology.

The gearshift has colorful buttons, the steering wheel is made of wood and white leather, and the logo on the front of the wheel lights up.

I have to focus back on the objective of getting to know him instead of being blown away by all the fancy.

"Alright, you ready?" He kindly asks me.

"Yes, I like to pray before leaving my home." I tell him.

"Ok, let's pray." He says.

And we grab each other's hands.

"Thank You Lord, for being ever present, the watcher, and the protector. We believe in You being the source of us having a good time tonight, of You leading the way tonight, and having Your will being the move tonight. We honor and praise you. Amen."

"Amen." He says back.

"I really enjoy hearing you pray; I know how powerful it is." He says as he pulls out of the parking spot and goes out to the street.

"Thank you; it is my favorite thing to do with God. He hears, and His promises are yes and amen, so I might as well talk and ask him for it, and by His will it will align." I say to him.

"Your faith is beautiful. I'm so glad I met someone who knows how deep faith is and how it's key." He softly says.

"Yes, that's right." I say back to him.

We both look at each other and smile.

I see the drive on the GPS is about 47 minutes. So, I sit back comfortably in the chair, taking in something new.

"How you feeling?" He asks me.

"I feel good, you? I ask him.

"Yes." He says it with a smile.

We enjoy the ride while the music plays softly in the background.

I started to wonder if I should ask him where we were having dinner, but I wanted to be surprised.

I trust his lead.

We arrive at a place called George's Mediterranean.

I quickly grab my phone to text Ashley the name and say that I'm good.

The restaurant already has a line. It is a huge, beautiful building.

The brick design is laid out all around the structure, and there are starry lights hanging from the top.

'Yummy Mediterranean food." I say it aloud, breaking the silence.

"The food here is great; have you been here before?" He asks me as he pulls up to the valet section.

"No first time." I say to him surely.

"Ok cool, my good friend owns the place, and I'm one of the food critics/junky." He says.

"I can't wait to eat." I say to him.

I love food, too; I saved my appetite after eating Wing Stop earlier.

We get to the front of the line, and the valet man opens the door for me.

Omega gets out and meets me on my side; he gives me a smile and then hands the keys to the driver and thanks him.

We walk shoulder to shoulder. I'm keeping to his pace, which gets us to sync into a rhythm as we walk up to the front of the restaurant door.

I didn't even take in much of the scenery and ambiance because my attention was so caught on Omega.

When we reach the door, he walks a little ahead of me to open it for me.

He looks at me with a smile.

"Thank you." I tell him as I walk past him.

The restaurant is beautiful.

We then walk up to the front desk, and Omega gives his name to our table.

We're walked to our table immediately by the host.

Omega pulls out my chair.

And we smile more at each other.

"Your server will be right with you, and so will Chef Uke." The host says this before walking off.

"Please tell me about yourself. I'm excited to get to know you." Omega says.

I'm feeling nervous; what should I say?

"Well, I just turned 25, I'm from Cali, I'm in the slow process of becoming an elementary school teacher, and I'm all about the will of God." I replied to him.

"My parents live in Berkeley; they have been married for 35 years. Dad served in the military for a couple years, then was diagnosed with pancreatic cancer and never fully recovered. My mom mostly takes care of him. He's a good man and did all he could to keep the family together. My sister and I just found our own routes to take, which led her to Texas and me here in the suburbs of Cali." I continue to say.

"I love people and my family and want to help the children, build the church up, and bring the light." I go on to say.

"I see it; I can tell you're not an average person, and you're carrying something big." He responds.

"Thank you." I sweetly replied.

"Tell me about you." I ask him in return,

"I'm 29 and from Tennessee; I visit there as often as I can. My parents moved to Texas when I was young to open a software business, but they're here in Cali now. I was an only child up until I was 20 when my parents had Maximum, my young brother, who passed away." He tells me.

"Yes, I'm sorry about that." I respond to him with sympathy.

"Thank you. It has been the hardest experience to deal with. I have been in and out of myself about it. It happened when I was on a food critique trip in Mexico. My parents were mad I wasn't there and told me how much they hated my career for it. We're getting back to an understanding, but it's been difficult." He tells me.

"Your family is in my prayers. How long have you been a food critic?" I ask him.

"Since I was 22, my grandpa opened a food truck, and I did videos covering each food item we sold, and people loved the commentary. Other food trucks asked me to do the same, then restaurants, and then I started my own business with it." He explains.

"Wow, that's amazing. Was Tokyo a stop for you when you were there for ramen?" I asked him.

"Yes." He says it with a smile.

"I made it to the international level; it's great; God has been good. I've been able to help my family and other people too. Started many food banks through it." He says.

"I know I found my purpose." He said, smiling.

I love to see happiness, especially on the face of a black man.

Our evening continued with smiles, laughter, and the good food that was prepared for us with special instructions by Omega and the Chef.

He prayed over the food.

"Thank You, God, for bringing us together tonight, celebrating something new, where we talk about You, our family, and our purposes over some great food. Please have this food nourish in wholesomeness, and allow us to bring honor to You any way we can. Amen."

"Amen." I respond.

"What a great prayer," I tell him.

I got the beef sauté, and he ordered the chicken sauté with rice and a Gyro split down the middle.

The meat was delicious, the sides were delicious, and the Gyro was beyond amazing with Tzatziki sauce. All are made fresh from a family recipe.

We both looked up at one another, smiling over our food and laughing at each other's mess.

I didn't even care for the spills I was making; I felt comfortable, and I felt that he was even more comfortable seeing me comfortable.

The strawberry lemonades were also so fresh, and we both agreed that we weren't interested in drinking alcohol tonight.

"Oh, the great guy Omega, how did you and your special lady enjoy the prepared dish?" Chef George Uke asks as he comes out of the kitchen with a huge smile.

"We were both talking about how good every bite of it was, Uke." Omega says as he stands up to shake his hand and greet him.

"Miss, this is such a great man; he has been a part of my food tasting critiques so many times, bringing crowds and crowds of people in here. People of all kinds. He knows people and food; what a combo!" Chef Uke shouts with joy.

I smile to see how happy Omega has seemed to make people.

And Chef Uke is right; food and people are a great combo.

"Thank you for the great food and atmosphere, Chef Uke. I'm already looking forward to coming back." I tell him.

"Thank you, beautiful lady; please do." He nicely responds.

Omega comes around to my side of the table to grab my hand so we can walk out.

I'm so happy and pleased and feel special with his gentleness and for showing me a great time.

We walk through the restaurant court to the entrance.

We meet the valet to pull Omega's car up to us.

Omega tips him and then opens the door for me. He gets into the car, and we head out.

"Wow, I'm so full." He says, grabbing his stomach.

"Yes, me too." I say to him while I put my head back in the seat.

The seats are so comfortable.

"You want any desert?" He looks over to ask me.

"Do you also critique deserts?" I ask him.

We both start laughing.

"I could never get that far; I was always too full." He says this while still laughing.

"I can imagine." I tell him.

"Well, I can share something sweet with you." I say to him with a smile.

We look at each other with a deep gaze.

We really are too full, but don't want the night to end.

I know we both feel how sweet this moment is.

"Yes, I can definitely share something sweet with you." He says back.

We look deep into each other's eyes again.

The connection is so deep with just a glance.

He breaks contact to look into his phone.

"Do you like funnel cakes? I know a place near the coast." He asks me.

"Yes, that sounds great, I haven't had one in awhile." I tell him

We smile and head out. The drive is so nice through the city, with the building lights, then hitting the coast.

I grab my phone to check in with Ashley.

I see all her texts.

"Have fun, girl."

"That place is delicious."

"He picked a good place."

"I know he's going to hook you up; Nick says he was a critique host there."

"Love you, girl."

I texted her back.

"Hey Ash, I'm having fun; the food was good, and we're going for dessert. Love you."

I put my phone away because I'm enjoying it, and at this moment, I'm in it way too much for any kind of technology.

Plus, he hasn't had his phone out all night.

The music is still playing softly in the background. And we continue to enjoy each other's company even in the silence as he drives.

We arrive, and the funnel cake shop is right off the coast before the pier.

I see a couple of other people in front.

"Ready?" He asks me as he shuts off the car.

"Yes." I say it with a smile.

He gets out, walks over, and opens the door for me.

We walk shoulder to shoulder to the front of the line.

"What would you like?" He asks.

"I love it with strawberries on top." I tell him.

"Ok gotcha." He replies with a smile.

He ordered, and they began to prepare the funnel cake.

You can see the bakers preparing it from scratch through the stand.

It already looks so good.

He grabs our plate and two forks.

We sit at a nearby bench and enjoy the night breeze and the scene of people passing by.

We engage in more conversation about church, our lives, and our love for helping people.

Once we're done, we head back to the car.

"I guess it's time I have to take you back home, beautiful lady." He says it graciously.

"Yes, I had so much fun with you, Omega; I smiled all night." I tell him as he walks to the car.

"Me too; this was great, and I was happy to see you smile." He says.

I get in the car as he gets in, too.

We make our way back through the city, finally reaching the suburbs.

We pull up to my apartment, and he gets out to open the door for me.

We then head to the elevator.

"I'll see you again soon?" He asks me

"Yes." I said, smiling at him.

We get to the top floor and walk down the hall to my front door.

He reaches in and embraces me with a big hug. This was the contact I was looking forward to all night.

The hug was tight and warm, and I felt I could stay there with him all night.

"Goodnight, Sunday." He says as he lets go.

"Goodnight." I wave and walk into my apartment.

It is 2:30 a.m., and I feel so awake.

I wash my face, take a shower, put my pajamas on, and get into bed.

I let Ashley know I'm home, and I'll call her and tell her all about it tomorrow.

My phone starts to ring as I set it down on my nightstand.

It's Omega.

"Hello," I answer.

"Hey, I just wanted to say thank you again for the night and to sleep well." He says

I smile.

"Thank you for everything, and I'm looking forward to seeing you again." I tell him.

"Ok, I'm about to pass out; I'll talk to you tomorrow." He says.

I can tell by the tone of his sleepy voice.

"Same, I'll talk to you tomorrow." I respond before hanging up the phone.

Thank You, Lord, for such a gentle soul.

I get on my knees to pray.

"Dear Lord, thank You for keeping us safe and leading us tonight. I feel blessed. I pray that You show up in this new relationship in

every way. Please show all that is not You. I want this to be centered on Your will. I will only keep moving for You. Amen."

I get into bed and feel covered by God's grace.

Thank You, Lord.

CHAPTER 16
The First Search

I wake up to my 8 a.m. alarm. I feel rested, but I could use some more sleep.

I use the restroom and then get on my knees to say my morning prayer.

"Good morning, Lord. Thank You for waking me up and giving me another day to live out Your will. Help me to be a blessing to others. Thank You. I love You. Amen."

I go to check my phone and see notifications from my emails and a text from the search group for Rebecca Meyers.

I grab my laptop and head to the kitchen. I checked my email first; hopefully, there was a message from the school board.

I thought I would have gotten a call back from my last voicemail on Saturday morning.

I then began to read the text from the group thread for the Rebecca Meyers search team I signed up for.

I scroll through more emails, and I don't see anything from the teacher's administration.

Maybe I should call again, I think to myself.

I'll pray about it and let God guide that part.

I check my news feeds and see that the family of Rebecca Meyers is still asking for anyone to come forth, even with the smallest information. A $10,000 reward has been offered.

I scroll through the text messages of all the people willing to help with the search.

There seem to be dozens of numbers I don't know.

I responded that I would be there at noon today to help with the first search.

I'll be going solo; Ashley and Nick have some things to do.

My phone started ringing, and I saw it was Omega calling.

I start to blush.

"Hello," I say as I answer the phone.

"Hey, good morning." He responds.

"Good morning, how are you?" I ask him.

"I'm doing well just getting up; how about you?" He then asks me.

"I'm pretty good; I'm just going to make some breakfast." I tell him.

"That sounds good. What are your plans today?" He asks me.

I didn't mention much about the Rebecca Meyers investigation last night on our date, but I'm sure he's heard about the news.

"I'm going to the search team for Rebecca Meyers. Have you heard about her?" I ask him.

He was quiet for a short time.

Maybe he hasn't heard of her.

"Ya, I heard about it; it's a sad story. That's cool, you're going to help." He says it quickly.

"Ya, the story has been pulling on me since it happened. I felt like I wanted to do all I could to help her family." I tell him.

"That's real dope of you." He responds.

I think maybe I should ask if he wants to join me.

"Well, when you get some time, let me know, and I would like to make more plans with you." He continues to say.

"Okay, the search starts at 12 p.m., and I think it's going on till it starts to get dark." I tell him.

"Okay, hit me up later; be safe." He responds.

"Okay, thanks; I will." I say this before hanging up the phone.

I guess this is a solo activity.

I grab some eggs to make my famous omelet and toast.

I prepare my food with gospel music playing in the background.

My ministry group chat texted me, notifying me that we have a new member.

"Yes, that's great; we'll be sure to introduce them on Sunday." I reply.

Whenever we receive new members into the group, we celebrate them with an entry scripture and brunch at the church.

I'm so excited for Garden Ministries to be growing the way it is.

I would have invited Rebecca Meyers to the group if I had known her sooner.

God and coming together to celebrate, have been a token of gathering lost individuals seeking higher righteousness in the Savior.

I go to my room, put some jeans on, and my T-shirt says, "I belong to Jesus."

I then put on my Nikes.

The time is near for the gathering for the search for Rebecca Meyers.

I pray as I walk out the door.

"Lord, please guide this search, bring us close to You, and reveal anything that may help.. Please have Your peace come upon the Meyers family. We all need You at this time, and we trust in Your word and salvation. Amen"

I grab my keys and head down to my car.

GPS says it's a 35-minute drive. We'll be looking out in some country hills, where her car was last seen.

I called Ashley to let her know I'll be out searching for most of the day.

"Hey girl," Ashley says when answering the phone.

"Hey Ash, what are you up to?" I ask her while connecting my phone to my car's Bluetooth speaker.

"I'm getting ready to go with Nick to the city to meet with some new investors." She speaks.

"Yes, that's so good; congrats to y'all." I tell her.

I'm so glad it's working for them; they deserve this.

"Thanks; that means so much. Nick is so happy; he's been singing all morning. And we have to thank you and Omega for making our official first job." She says it excitedly.

I think of Omega, and I smile to myself.

"How was the date last night, girl? Give me some brief details, and we can really gush later." She says.

"It was great; he's so sweet, and I love his passion for his work and the Lord. We had dessert and enjoyed each other's company, which was simple and honest. I felt comfortable." I tell her honestly.

"So sweet; I love that. I'm so glad about all that's happened." She says.

"Me too, girl! I feel God, and I have prayed about it every step of the way. And I'm glad to have my friends in my corner." I tell her.

"Yes, always, girl." She responds.

"I'm on my way to the first search group for Rebecca Meyers." I tell her.

"Oh, yes, I remember that was happening today. How are you feeling about all of it?" She asks me.

"I'm happy to help and trying to stay in hope that something will be revealed. The space has been marked off for weeks and on watch by the police until the search party was officially organized. So, they really believe there is some evidence out there; they just need all the help available." I tell her.

"Yeah, girl, hoping for all good things. And that her family gets some peace." She says.

"Yes, I hope so too." I tell her.

I want this done for her family before it becomes a spectacle.

The news has a way of making the victim look like a terrible person, especially if they don't get any information soon.

"When do you plan on seeing Omega again?" Ashley asks.

"He wants to do something soon. Told me to call when I get free time after this." I tell her.

I get a leap of excitement just thinking about seeing him again.

"Yes, get it Sunday." She shouts with excitement.

She's my fan girl.

I laugh with her.

"Also, Destiny called and said we had another member join Garden Ministries, so we have to put together the celebration package for Sunday service." I tell her.

"That's great. I'm so happy it's growing like this." She says.

"Me too, girl; God is good." I say.

"All the time." She replies.

"Okay, girl, I'm going to go and get to the search. I am praying for a successful business day for you and Nick." I tell her.

"Thanks, bestie, and also praying for a successful day with the search." She replies.

"Okay, love you, girl. Be safe." I reply.

"You too love you, bye." The phone hangs up and goes right back to my gospel music.

Twenty minutes out from the searching ground now.

I soon arrived at the location and saw multiple cars parked along the designated area.

I get out and walk closer to the grounds.

"Lord, please let Your spirit prevail here." I speak to myself.

I reach the top of the hill and see the multitude of people; it looks to be more than the dozen I seen within the group chat.

It is amazing that so many people came out.

Within range, I don't see anyone I know.

The search organizer puts everyone in small group sections to cover the land. I follow the directions and head to the bottom hillside with the rest of the group.

A group leader is assigned to each group, whom we are to report to if we find something, and for them to follow up with the main leader.

As we gather we share our concerns and thoughts about the case with each other.

I then asked if my group and I could pray before we searched.

Everyone agrees, and we all come together and hold hands.

I pray, *"Heavenly Father, thank You for gathering these individuals for a great cause to find Your lost child. We pray for revelation, Your guidance, and peace. Please keep us safe and hold Rebecca Meyers family. We love You and thank You for Your grace. Amen"*

The group all says Amen.

We disperse, and we search.

We were provided water and chips.

There was so much to cover; thank God so many people came to help.

When it came time to close the search, everyone from all the groups headed back up the hill.

Our group didn't find anything, but another group did find what looked to be her shoe.

The heaviness has come upon the whole search group.

The police were on sight to gather the evidence.

People are crying out; I gather with a couple of other girls for us all to mourn and pray together.

As the heaviness eases, everyone starts to head back to their cars.

I make it to my car, finally exhale, and begin to head home.

I check my phone and see texts from Ashley and Omega.

I decide to just head home and then I'll reach out to them once I'm there.

My ride home is quick, with my gospel music playing softly in the background.

I decided to get some Chick-fil-A for dinner.

I made it home safely, thank God.

I get to my apartment, eat my food, and then take a long, hot shower.

The news will be released soon, and everyone will be saddened by the new information.

I text Omega back, letting him know all is well and of the findings from the search.

He sends sweet, encouraging text messages throughout the rest of the night, letting me know his day was good and that I was on his mind.

I also texted Ashley back, letting her know of the news.

After my conversations with them both, I started to feel myself getting tired and got on my knees to say my nightly prayer.

"God, I thank You for being the Almighty, where we can put our worries, hurts, and fears in Your hands. I look to You for comfort for us all and the Meyers family. I thank You for Your grace and for sending me to the search today. I ask You to cover over my friends tonight—the ones I have had for some time and the new ones I have made. You really are love, and I thank You for drawing us all close together. I praise You. Amen."

I lay in bed and went to sleep for the night.

CHAPTER 17
Mega Eating

I wake up with gratitude in my heart.

After the new evidence, I know news outlets will be circulating around it today.

I get on my knees to begin my morning prayer.

"Good morning, Father. Thank You for waking me and watching over me as I rest. I seek You today and am getting closer to Your heart. Use me and continue to reveal what You want through me. My day is already full of joy and peace because I have You. Amen."

I grab my phone to see multiple headlines concerning Rebecca Meyers and texts from Ashley, Omega, and the search group.

I see email notifications, hopefully, something from the school board. No new calls from the school administration.

I make an easy avocado toast for breakfast, and I call Omega.

I feel the exciting nerves tending with each ring.

"Hey Sunday," he says, answering the phone.

"Good morning, Omega." I say to him.

"How are you?" He asks me.

"I'm doing pretty well; I just made some breakfast and am planning my day." I tell him.

"How was your breakfast? What did you make?" He asks me.

"I just had some avocado toast and made a cappuccino." I tell him.

"Sounds good. I ate a big plate of eggs and bacon." He tells me.

"That sounds good too. How's your morning going?" I ask him.

"It's cool; I finished working out and some other business calls." He says.

"Productive morning." I respond to him.

"Yes, it has to be." He says.

"So, is there any chance we can get together today?" He goes on to ask me.

"That sounds good; what were you thinking?" I ask him.

"Can I maybe come get you, and you can come with me to check out some new places for food tasting?" He asks me.

"Yeah, that sounds like fun." I tell him.

I'm excited to get into his world and to have my heart take a break from the hard work of discovering new leads with the Rebecca Meyers case and worrying about the teaching position.

"What's a good time to pick you up?" He asks me.

"Maybe in about 2 hours," I tell him.

"Okay, that sounds good. I'll let you know when I'm on the way." He says.

"Okay, see you soon." I say to him

"Alright, bye Sunday," he says.

"Bye." I say this before hanging up.

I'm looking forward to this.

I eat quickly before I get into the shower.

I put on some easy-wearing denim jeans and a white T-shirt that says "Represent for God".

I put on my sparkly sandals and do an easy touch of makeup.

About an hour and a half later my phone starts ringing. I answer when I see it's Omega.

"Hello."

"Hey Sunday, I just wanted you to know I'm on the way. Like 10 minutes from your place." He tells me.

"Okay, that sounds good. See you soon." I tell him.

"Alright, see you soon." He tells me

It feels like time is already flying by.

I soon hear my doorbell ring.

I open the door to see his smiling and welcoming face. He looks very handsome in his light jeans, red Jordans, and red shirt.

His long curls were hanging loose.

And he's carrying a beautiful bouquet of roses.

"Hey, how are you? You look beautiful." He says as he comes in for a hug.

"Thank you. I'm doing good, you?" I ask while in his embrace.

"Are you ready?" He asks me.

"Yes." I tell him as I grab my purse, set the vase with the roses down on the counter, and lock my front door.

We head to his car, and I see that he's in his truck today, which is just as luxurious and beautiful as the Benz.

The interior and exterior are both clean.

I'm impressed with his cleanliness, it's attractive in every way.

Thank You, God; that's on my list of great characteristics.

"I appreciate you coming along with me. I have a couple of tasting stops to make. There having me come in before the restaurants open tonight." He tells me as he starts to take off.

"Really? That's cool. Do you know what you'll be tasting?" I ask him.

"No, not yet." He responds to me.

"That can be exciting, a surprise, and something new." I tell him.

"Yes, it'll be fun with you." He says this while looking over and smiling.

The drive there is almost an hour, but we soon make it.

We enjoyed small conversations and music.

Omega and I went and tasted many different foods throughout the day.

We had Italian, Mediterranean, African, Spanish, different appetizers, and amazing beverages.

He really does have one of the best jobs in the world.

All the chefs thought highly of him, and Omega was always so generous and humble with his kind words.

It really is so great to see a young black man with many great connections who are more like friends, and he, too, in return, shows such humility and respect.

We managed to gather what would be extra food for his "Mega Eating" foundation to help the youth, homeless, and poverty-driven people.

We also gathered some to donate to the church.

All of it was such a blessing.

He maintained being so respectful and gentlemanly throughout the day.

Everyone was so kind, and we all prayed over each meal we ate.

Omega and I had great conversations throughout the day, getting to know each other better.

I told him all about Garden Ministries, and he told me all about Mega Eating and the big plans we had.

He managed to open up more about his family and losing his younger brother, which was the result of a hit-and-run.

They are still looking for the suspect.

I told him about waiting for my new teaching job and how they still haven't called, and he gave me some encouraging words, saying, "All I can do is wait in God's time."

He's experiencing waiting, too, as a suspect comes forward for the loss of his brother.

I tell him how I've kept my attention on the Rebecca Meyers case and the discovery while on the search yesterday to keep my mind off the teaching job.

Since we found such evidence, there is no need to conduct more searches.

I told him about the love I curated for Rebecca and how I would have hoped to draw her to Garden Ministries.

We finish up at the different restaurants in the city, all full and enjoying each other's company.

Ashley and Nick called and told us about the good news of new investors, and they'll be able to get some driving jobs tonight.

We all thank each other for the help.

God has really brought us together; I feel his peace, I feel his grace, and I also feel His pull to something new, something to discover here.

The day has gone, and we decide to settle at a rooftop restaurant, enjoying the last views of the sunset.

We managed to make more plans for another date and share a desert.

We walk so close shoulder to shoulder all throughout the day, and as the night ends and it's time to head home, I'm already missing his presence.

I must maintain myself; I can't fall so hard so fast for God's child. Only in His time, and we have plans soon, so I must rest in that, no need to get anxious.

After the peaceful drive home, he walks me up to my apartment and hugs me goodnight.

I get inside and get comfortable in my pajamas, texting Omega goodnight.

I get on my knees to say my prayers before bed.

"Father, thank You for the day. Thank You for showing up and protecting us, providing, and being our guide during the day. I ask You to search me, our Lord, to purify my heart and continue to lead me in the direction You want me in this new relationship. Please watch over all my friends and family tonight. I love You. Amen."

I get into bed and instantly fall asleep.

CHAPTER 18: Dinner and Revelation

I have spent the past three weeks enjoying lunch and dinner dates with Omega.

He has become a member of the church and of Garden Ministries.

We went on a double date with Ashley and Nick and had the best time.

God has been so good at keeping the relationship pure that Omega hasn't pressed on me or tried to convince me of anything sexually.

We had our first kiss after seeing a movie, and it was deeper and more passionate than I ever thought a first kiss could be.

I'm falling for him, and the way he looks at me makes me feel safe, adored, and honest.

I feel that he has really taken himself aside to get to know me, and I'm ready to share more.

I'm going to make my famous chicken parmigiana for him tonight.

I'm so excited to cook for him, to be at home relaxing, watching a movie, and sharing the intimacy of my home with him.

My phone rings, and I see his name on the screen.

I answer the phone. "Hello."

"I'll be there real soon; are you sure you don't need me to bring anything?" He asks.

"No, thank you, and I'll see you soon." I respond.

"Okay, bye," he says.

"Bye." I say this before hanging up.

I put on a pretty red dress and did my hair in an upward style as the front curls hung.

I hear the knock on the door.

He's here; I go to answer it, and I'm greeted with a huge bouquet of red roses and a hug.

"These are beautiful." I tell him while looking at the biggest, fullest bouquet yet.

He hasn't failed at bringing the best bouquets to me; he knows I love flowers and brings them all the time.

My whole apartment is full of them, from my bedroom, front room and anywhere else I can put them.

He even brings them to the ministry to support its title, Garden Ministries.

He really does have it looking like a garden in my apartment and in the church's recreational room, where we hold our Garden Ministries services.

He looks handsome in jeans and a Nike T-shirt.

With a pair of Nike shoes to match.

"Wow, it smells great in here." He tells me sweetly.

"Thank you; I'm glad to make you something to eat." I tell him,

"Thanks Sunday." He says, then grabs my chin and leads my face up for a kiss.

Passion was felt.

"Are you hungry now? I have little appetizers to hold us over; the food is almost done." I tell him.

"Yes, please bring it out." He says this while grasping his hands in excitement.

I know he loves food.

He sits on the bar stool as I lay out some dips, chips, cheese, crackers, and salami for appetizers.

I also serve him fresh, squeezed lemonade.

I got a bottle of wine to serve with the main dish.

The evening got more beautiful; I added candles with some light music playing in the background.

I served us chicken parmigiana, and we both had second rounds of food.

We laughed throughout dinner.

I have chocolate chip cookies, which I baked earlier for dessert, but right now, I don't think we will be eating them.

"That was so good Sunday, thank you. I really appreciate you cooking dinner tonight. And you can really throw down." He says this while we sit back on the couch.

"Thanks baby." I quickly covered my mouth after realizing what I had said.

I called him 'baby,' and it slipped out.

He puts his hand on my leg and starts giggling.

"Yo, it's okay; you're my baby too." He tells me.

"You're my beautiful baby, and I really like you." He says.

I look into his sweet eyes, and I see his honesty.

I go to grab his hand.

"Thank you, baby." I shyly replied.

I have been worried about moving too fast, but this has felt good as if everything has been done right on time.

We scrolled through the TV channels until we settled on watching The Office.

I don't have many streaming services because I don't get into modern television due to all the misinformation it displays.

Usually, too much sex, addiction, witchcraft, and other sinful behavior.

I had to let go of what I watched, what I allowed into my soul, and what I sold myself into.

I changed all the intake, such as food, entertainment, and people, that didn't resemble God.

And I feel the difference in my life; I feel God has planted me, to get me molded and pruned to fit into the perfect image that He sees in me.

It starts with allowing God to be my main source, and I make sure to go to Him with everything.

As Omega and I get closer, I feel that I must give this new relationship to God as well.

My phone notifies me, and I pick it up to check. I haven't looked at my phone all night because I've been enjoying myself and just want to be in Omega's presence.

I see the headline is about Rebecca Meyers. I haven't really talked to Omega about it.

"Everything good?" He asks me as I scroll through the story on my phone.

"Yeah, it's just that these stories about Rebecca Meyers are so sad. There are no current leads on the suspect, and they are leaning towards an unsolved homicide since we found her shoe in the hills." I tell him sadly.

I see him shift to come closer to me, but I also feel him tense up too.

"Yeah, that whole story is so messed up." He says it passively.

"I get so much information on it; I know these things can't be rushed; I just wanted some news to move forward and settle that sadness in my soul and the family." I tell him.

"Something has me so pulled for her and the whole story since day one." I continue to say.

"Well…" Omega begins to say, and I can tell he's nervous.

I sense he's trying to say something to me.

I sit quietly, waiting for him to finish what he's trying to say.

"I know of her being with an old homeboy of mine right before she disappeared." He comes out to say.

We sit in long silence.

"What, really?" I finally managed to say.

I shift my body up at this new information.

"What, who, what happened?" I just have so many questions.

He's quiet for a bit longer.

"I don't talk to him anymore; his name is Cain. He was bringing Rebecca around, and they started to get dark and more into drugs and other shit I wasn't feeling. I needed to stay away because I wanted to get out of the scene and stop heavy drinking." He tells me.

He's sitting stiffer. I can tell he's uncomfortable now.

"Omega, you know about the last person she may have been with?" I ask him.

He nods his head.

My mind races with thoughts, and my heart is beating so fast.

This whole time, he knew something, and it seemed to be the lead that needed to solve the case.

I feel like I'm spinning. The man I'm falling for seems to have a huge part of the information for the case.

I don't know what to say.

The whole room went silent. I look over at him, and I see that he looks sad.

I felt that I have been getting to know him well, and I know that he is so kind and honest and is really after knowing God, giving God the glory, and having God's light shine through him.

My heart deepens for him; I know there must be more to this revelation.

"Can you tell me more about what happened?" I settle to ask him.

He clears his throat up to speak.

"He would bring her around to parties more and more; they would get high and do their thing. I never knew much about her; he kept it really low-key. And I had to stay away because I didn't want that scene anymore. And he changed and got dark. I couldn't be around it." He tells me.

I'm still shocked by what I'm hearing.

"I haven't seen him since a little before she went missing." He tells me.

"And I'm sorry about all of this and not saying anything about it." He continues.

"Why haven't you said anything before?" I ask him.

"I was thinking selfishly because I know they're going to look into me, taking me in. Since I have this information and neither one of them is around, everyone is looking for someone to blame." He says.

"Plus, I didn't want you to hate me." He continues.

I don't know what to say or think.

I know I feel for him, but I'm still spinning with this.

I need air, so I stand up to get some space.

He stands up behind me.

"Sunday I'm so sorry, baby. I should have said something. I have been all over the place, letting the drinking go and losing my baby brother, trying to keep the company. I just don't know." He says.

I see the tears forming in his eyes.

"I know Omega; it's just that she's missing and gone, and it seems you know a great deal." I tell him.

"I know, and I have been scared of what will happen." He responds.

I start having a moment of understanding. He has lost a life close to him, such as Rebecca's family, and her habits and shortcomings weren't able to be resolved like Omega is trying to do with his life.

And I do understand when he says they will hold him as the suspect in this case. He's a black man and may have been the last one to know what was really going on, and their family is ready for someone to blame.

"I'm going to make this right, okay?" He says it quickly.

"I have been trying to make it right in my head, and meeting you has made me feel that I can get a chance to forget the hurt all of this will cause. But I'm going to do what's right. I want you to know that I am really that honest man; you have gotten to know." He's saying with tears rolling down his face.

I look so confused. I know this can go so badly for him, but I know he must take this lead for justice.

"I told you everything, all that I know." He says.

We are standing face-to-face, and I do believe in him; I just don't know what to say.

“Okay, let’s just end the night, so things can be cooled down,” I tell him.

“Okay, I’ll go.” I tell him.

I see him getting himself together to leave; I would have liked for a longer time. I just don’t want to go back and forth with this for the rest of the night.

I need to figure out what to do now.

I honestly can’t deny the pull of feelings I have.

And I honestly do know that I care about him a lot, and I don’t want to lose him to this or anything at that.

I walk him to the door.

He turns to look at me at the entrance of the door.

“I really am sorry, Sunday.” He says.

I start to tear up, and I feel myself choking on those tears.

“I like you, Omega, and I think we should figure something out about this.” I tell him.

“I just feel tired and need to come together with God about it, but I also think you shouldn’t have to carry all of this.” I continue.

“And I’m tired too.” He manages to say.

“Get some rest, and I’m just going to talk with God and sleep too.” He continues.

“Okay, sounds good.” I tell him.

We go in for a hug, and he kisses me on the forehead.

I give him a gentle smile.

I close the door, head to my room, wash my face, put my pajamas on, and get on my knees to pray. I begin to instantly cry, and I cry out to God.

He knows me, my tears, my confusion, and the pain I'm feeling.

One of the best parts of the heavenly Father is that all you have to do is cry out His name, and He'll know what you need.

I then get into bed and roll over to sleep.

CHAPTER 19
Between You, Me, and God

I spent the next three days reading into God's word day and night.

I did some writing and meditation.

I got into worshipping God.

I needed more than ever to hear His voice and His whispers.

I need His presence to move through my place, through my heart, and through Omega's as well.

I need His confirmation and mostly His guidance.

I have started to fall in love with Omega, a man who is so respectful and has shown himself to be a good leader and follower of Christ. Then I'm hit with horrid news, but I want to protect Omega rather than expose what he has shared.

I'm looking for God's light and hand in this situation.

Omega has called through the past couple of days, checking in and apologizing.

Ashley has sensed my distance and questioned my relationship with Omega.

I've wanted to keep this revelation between God, Omega, and me, so I have brushed her questions off and told her I've been feeling under the weather.

I'm still moved to be in Omega's life, and I feel God doesn't deny our relationship; He has called him into my life for such a time as this.

So, I want to seek God with Omega and try to discover the best way to shine God's light through this situation.

It was a situation that turned out to involve us both, but since we both love God, and want to do what's right, there is a way through this.

There is always a way through.

With You, God, it is already worked out. We just have to seek You for the pathway.

I have been hibernating for the past three days, sitting in complete silence except for answering a few phone calls so that people know I'm okay.

Tomorrow is Sunday, and Omega has tried to make Sunday service with me every week.

Sometimes, he has an early morning meeting for his Mega Eating Foundation on Sundays, but other than that, he always tries to make church service with me.

I don't want to stop that.

I also want to talk to him before service tomorrow, so there isn't any tension flowing.

I go to grab my phone after sitting in my worship area to call Omega.

"Hey Sunday." He kindly says as he answers the phone.

My heart always flutters at the sound of his voice saying my name.

"Hi Omega." I responded.

"How are you? I'm happy to hear from you." He asks.

"I'm doing pretty well; how about you?" I ask him in return.

"I'm alright; I've just been taking care of some things." He says.

"I was wondering if we could get together soon? Do you have any plans tonight?" I ask him.

"I don't have anything going on tonight, so it would be great to see you." He tells me.

I think it would be best to continue this conversation in the privacy of one of our homes.

"Do you maybe want to come to my place, and we talk here?" I go on to ask him.

"Ya, sure, I can come there to you." He tells me.

"Okay, great, I'll be here for the rest of the day, so when you're ready, come." I respond to him.

"Okay, cool, I'll get ready to head over soon." He says.

"I'll see you soon then." I tell him.

"Okay, bye Sunday." He says this before we hang up.

I can't hold back the jumping excitement I feel, knowing I'll be seeing Omega soon.

I have lounged in a light pink sweatsuit throughout the day; my femineity still wants to look cute for him.

So, I also go and fluff my curls out.

I then put some chips and salsa and drinks out for us to snack on

About 35 minutes later, Omega texts me that he'll be pulling up in about 10 minutes.

I say a quick prayer before he gets here.

"God, I need You to be in the middle of Omega and me. I need You to interfere and take control of the new revelation here. As we come together to discuss a terrible matter, please guide us. You know our hearts and, most importantly, what we need. Amen."

The doorbell then rings.

I go to answer to see Omega standing with a bouquet of beautiful white roses.

He's wearing grey sweatpants and a red Nike shirt, looking very handsome.

His curls are hanging down and wild. I love his natural hair.

"Hey, Sunday." He says, coming in for a long, strong hug.

I missed this, feeling his strength.

We release, and he hands me the flowers.

I set the flowers up on the counter top.

I ran out of vases, but then he started to buy me the vases to go with the flowers.

"I'm glad to see you, Omega." I say it with a small smile.

We sit together on the kitchen stools.

I don't know where to begin, but I am led to start with God.

"Were you going to church tomorrow?" I ask him.

"Yes, I'll be going. What about you?" He asks me.

"Yes, always looking forward to church." I tell him.

We sat in silence and ate some of the chips and salsa I provided.

"I know we need to talk about Rebecca and the situation." He says, breaking the silence.

"I needed the past couple of days to settle into what you told me." I tell him.

"I know, and I appreciate you giving me the chance to explain." He responds.

"The guy's name is Cain; he was with Rebecca before she went missing. I met him through another homie at a party almost 3 years ago. He wasn't with Rebecca when I first met him. But a little over a week before she went missing, he was with her every single day; they were doing drugs and heavy drinking." He tells me.

"I'm not sure how they even met or if they knew each other before. My little brother died around that time, so I wasn't noticing things around me so deeply. He was trying to be there for me, but it was in the wrong way, always wanting to go drink it away or handle the situation with any means necessary." He continues.

"I was numb to it and ignored it a lot. I just remember that it didn't seem like that's where she wanted to be, always partying, but I guess she really liked Cain." He says.

He says with relief.

"Thanks for telling me. You know I've been following the case since it happened. I felt so connected and wanted to help any way I could." I tell him.

"It felt so close to me, and I couldn't understand why. So, I just got involved as much as I could. I remember when we did the search in the hills, people were angry and kept saying how someone knows something, whoever that person is, is so selfish, and the person she was with will pay for this. It got dark, but I met you, and it seemed to ease my mind and nerves from the sadness the case was bringing me. And then you also settled my question as to what could have happened when you told me the other night. In a way, my heart is settled by the mystery of her, and I sense that I can go on from it. I believe that's why I was so connected to all of this, because you were coming into my life." I will continue to say.

"There are a lot of angry people out there around this, though, very hostile, and I don't sense forgiveness in their hearts. But you're such a good man; I don't want them holding this on you until Cain comes out, and that's if he does." I explain as the tears build up.

"And so I do understand why you held back the information. And I just want you to know that I'm here for you, to help you get through all of this with God as our guide." I tell him.

"I don't want to lose you to this; it isn't your fault, but I can see how the world will hold you accountable." I finally say.

"Thank you, Sunday; it has been eating me up on what to say. And I have gone through the motions of just going to the authorities to say something. I've called Cain, and his phone is disconnected. And I don't know any more than what I told you. I know what that family is going through, though. My parents have worked on getting closer to God and each other after losing my little brother; they stopped worrying about the person at fault. My dad hired an investigator, but there hasn't been much information to share; the person just took off so fast. We have felt the best thing to do is go on healing. My mom is working on having to forgive someone she doesn't even know. I'm thankful for a family like that, but I can't say Rebecca's family is like that." He explains it to me.

"I know, and I'm so sorry for all this hurt. It's like the devil is throwing major darts. I know God hears us; we just have to keep asking what to do. Until then, I guess this will just be us, between us." I say to him.

"Okay." I see his tears coming in.

"Okay." I reach up for a hug.

And then we began kissing deeply, intimately.

We break free from the kiss, sharing a longing look into each other's eyes.

I still have to remain sustained for God.

And I realized we never had the conservation of me remaining a virgin until marriage.

I thought he would notice by my love and pressing in on God that I have to sustain myself till marriage.

Then again, he has never pressed me in such a way.

My mind is wandering everywhere.

"I don't have any food, but maybe we can order out." I tell him.

"Okay, that would be great." He responds.

We managed to enjoy the rest of our night, eating tacos and watching movies.

It felt like we made up for the time that was lost over the past couple of days.

Omega comes to help me clean up the rest of the mess in the kitchen.

Then he pulled me in for a kiss, and I felt the passion, the need, and the man in him.

I kissed him back with passion, enjoying the need in it, until I felt the pressing in, and I loosened up my grip.

He lets go, too, and gives me a smile.

"Soft lips and everything." He comments.

"Thank you." I say it with a giggle.

But I have to talk with him about sex.

"You make me feel great, and I love kissing you, Omega, but that is all I can do. I'm a virgin, and I'm staying that way until I'm married." I straight up told him.

He starts to smile really big and nods his head.

I'm trying to figure out what he's thinking.

"I knew that was the case, and I was never going to take it there. I think it's a beautiful thing, honorable, and even sexy." He says it with a giggle.

"I'm having my own journey with abstainment; for about the past 3 months, I haven't had sex." He tells me.

My head and heart increase in ease and peace. He really is special and changing his life.

I instantly felt the connection deepen. I finally ended things with Marcus three months ago, and so has Omega with his sin.

I believe Omega and I came to an agreement before we even met; this can really be the hand of God.

"That is beautiful to hear, Omega, and I know God's face is smiling upon us. So, we can focus on loving eachother and worshipping Him." I tell him.

I then noticed that I said the word love.

"I love you too, baby." He responds.

I'm trying to figure myself out and what to say.

"I was saying like the love of God and all we are going through." I try to fix what I'm saying.

But then again, maybe it is love; it's just so soon.

"I know what you were trying to say, but I'm saying I'm falling in love with you." He responds to me.

"I know everything seems soon, but I know what it is when it comes to you, and it's only going to get deeper." He explains,

"I feel the same way too." I tell him.

"Come here and let me hug you." He says as he pulls me in for a hug.

"Let's keep praying together, going to church, reading the Bible, doing whatever God wants of us, and seeing where this takes us." He says.

"Okay." I tell him with a kiss.

"So, I'm going to get going, but I'll see you at church in the morning. Did you want me to pick you up, baby?" He sweetly asks me.

"Yes, please, baby. Thank you." I respond.

"Of course." He says,

I walk him to the door, and he gives me another kiss goodnight before leaving.

I feel good.

I headed to take a shower and pick up my church dress for tomorrow.

I received a text from Omega saying that he made it home safely.

And I respond to Ashley's texts.

She's still concerned about my lack of communication, but I tell her I'm getting better and will be at church tomorrow.

I then get on my knees to say my final prayer for the night.

"Heavenly Father, thank You for watching over me throughout the day. Thank You for being You and being the God of justice and

peace, the One who will make this crooked path straight. Help me, help Omega to be more like Jesus, and as we journey on with what we know, please help us to make the right decisions to walk this out for Your glory. I love You. Amen."

CHAPTER 20
First Sunday and Family

I feel rested, and I wake up ready to go to church.

It's the first Sunday, so we get to do communion with the congregation.

This will be my first communion with Omega.

I say my morning prayers.

"Good morning, Father. Thank You for waking me up this morning. Thank You for another chance to give You glory, honor, and praise. I thank You that I get another day to live out your will for my life. Help me, Lord; help me to be a blessing for others. I love You. Amen."

I checked my phone and saw a good morning text from Omega. I reply to him and then head to the kitchen to eat a quick breakfast.

I'm not leading Bible study today, but I'll make sure to have my notepad and pen to take notes.

I call Ashley.

"Hey girl, good morning," Ashley says when answering the phone.

"Good morning, how are you?" I ask her as I put my berries in a bowl.

"I'm good, getting ready for church. How are you feeling?" She asks me.

I know she's been concerned because I've been keeping our conversation short the last couple of days.

I didn't let her know I was getting together with Omega last night.

"I'm good I'm getting ready for church too. Looking forward to the word today." I tell her.

"Same here; are you coming with Omega?" She asks me.

"Yes, he's picking me up." I tell her.

"Okay, let's all do lunch afterwards." She says.

"Okay, that sounds good, Ashley." I respond.

"Okay, see you soon, bye." She says this before hanging up.

Nick, Ashley, Omega, and I have had lunch a couple of times after church service; they were great double dates, and we always have a good time together.

After I eat breakfast, I go to my room and put my church dress on. I'm wearing a long cream-colored button-up dress.

I decide to tie my hair up, let my curls hang down from there, and then apply a light layer of makeup.

I hear my phone notify me of a text message; it's from my mom.

"Hi Sunday, your father and I want to come for a visit soon. We want to come sometime this coming week. We'll probably bring Granny too. We are headed to church. Love you."

I'm always happy to see my family; the last time we were all together was for my birthday.

I'll call her after church to pick a time for a visit.

My phone notifies me again with a text message from Omega.

He tells me he'll be here in 10 minutes.

I still jump with excitement at seeing him.

I can't wait to hug and kiss him.

Once I'm looking in the mirror, confirmed and ready, I hear his knock at the door.

I open the front door to see him standing tall with a nice button-up shirt on, a nice pair of dress shorts, and loafers.

He has his long curls neatly brushed back.

He always puts himself together and smells so amazing.

"Hey, my beautiful baby." He says as he pulls me in for a big hug, then pulls my chin up for a deep kiss.

"Hi, you look so good." I tell him after the kiss.

"Thanks, babe; you know I try to look sharp for God." He says it with a giggle.

"I know that's right. Okay, I'm going to just grab my Bible and notebook, and I'm ready." I tell him.

He smiles and nods.

Wow, he's just so handsome.

I grab my things, lock the front door, and we head to his car.

We enjoy the car ride there listening to R&B gospel.

The thought of what he revealed to me last night seeps in, but I tell myself I know that God will speak to me about this, and we'll know what to do.

He said yes after I asked him if he wanted to have lunch with Nick and Ashley after church.

We pull up to the church and park and see all the church members gathering.

Walking in, everyone always greets each other as they pass by. I love the peaceful, kind atmosphere of the church.

We make it to the rec room where Garden Ministries is held, and some of the group members are already there.

We have about 10 minutes until Bible study starts.

I see Nick and Ashley walk in and some more members.

Destiny, another member, is leading the Bible study this morning.

And she writes on the board, 'Jesus and His parables.'

This is going to be great; the conversation about the parables always teaches us something new.

After a great hour-long Bible study, everyone moves into the church hall for the sermon.

Pastor Millstone spoke on Philippians 4:13, "I can do all things through Christ who strengthens me."

The word was energizing, refreshing, pure, hopeful, and always just what I needed.

The congregation shouted and praised God throughout, and the choir sang with cheerful noise.

And we took communion all together.

After service, we socialized with other members and Pastor Millstone.

Pastor Millstone asked Nick and Omega if they were interested in sharing their testimonies for the "Man Can with God" service.

They both happily agreed.

It made Ashley and I so glad that they wanted to be a part of the event with some of the other men in the church.

I also started to think about how that could be tough for Omega, especially since he was just going through the loss of his little brother.

But then again, this is the best place to share and be vulnerable with the support of the church, pastor, and God.

We decided to eat out at the diner for lunch; it's near the church.

We all met up there and enjoyed lunch together, with good conversation and laughter.

Ashley kept telling Omega and me how glad she was that we were all together.

Nick's business is going well, and he's getting plenty of clients each day.

I'm thankful for my group of friends and the support we continue to pour into each other.

We hang out at the diner for another hour after finishing our meals; then, we get up to head home.

We all hugged each other goodbye, and Ashley told me she would text me later.

And I was reminded I must call my mom back.

Omega and I head back to my place, listening to more R&B gospel and feeling full from lunch.

"My mom, dad, and grandma want to come visit soon. She texted me before church this morning, so I'm going to call her back and plan that with her." I tell him as we cruise on the drive.

"They're in Berkeley, right?" He asks me.

"Yes, and they have more space at their home for a visit, but I know she wants to come to my place to see how I'm living. She's worried about my income and about getting a job before my inheritance runs out." I tell him.

"Ya, that sounds like a mom." He says as we both giggle.

"Well, God gave you that woman and family, so He built you to handle them. You're beautiful, you're smart, and you have a great heart; they can't deny that you'll be more than good." He tells me.

"Aww, wow, thanks, baby; that means so much." I tell him.

"It's true; I'm just glad you're in my life now." I will continue to say.

"Me too, baby." He says.

"No pressure, and you don't have to decide now, but if you want to come by when they're here, you're more than welcome." I say to him.

"Yeah, I would like that; just let me know." He says.

We smile at each other, and we soon make it back to my place.

He comes up to my apartment to hang out and watch a movie with me.

After he hugs and kisses me goodbye, I call my mom.

"Hey momma." I say this when she answers the phone.

"How are you? Me and your dad are here." She says.

"All is good, mom, home from church and getting ready for bed." I tell her.

"How are y'all doing?" I ask her.

"You must have gone out since you're just now getting home from church. How was service?" She asks.

"Church was good, and I went out to lunch with my friends afterwards. Tell dad I said hi." I tell her.

I started to think of Omega and how I would introduce him to my family.

We've already called each other baby and told one another about falling in love, but he hasn't officially asked me to be his girl.

I don't want to entertain that thought; no one can deny that we are together. I remember Nick telling me he didn't just date to have a girlfriend; he was looking for a wife.

My heart flutters at the thought.

"Oh, okay, how's Ashley and Nick?" She asks.

"They're both doing really well, mom; their relationship is good, and the business is going well." I tell her.

"That's good to hear for the both of them." She responds.

"There was also someone else at lunch with us; his name is Omega; he's more like my special friend." I tell her.

"Really? Okay Sunday. I didn't even know you met someone new." She says.

"Ya, it's been some time now since we've known each other. I've just been taking it easy with him." I tell her.

"Well, are we going to meet him?" She asks.

"Yes, he already said he wants to meet you all." I tell her.

"Okay good. And how's the job search going Sunday?" She asks me.

"It's going, mom. I'm going to have a fresh start starting tomorrow, making some calls." I tell her.

"Okay then, let me know if you need anything." She says.

"I will, mom, thanks. When did y'all want to come over?" I ask her.

"What's a good day for you this week?" She asks.

"How about Wednesday?" I say to her.

"Okay, I'm going to bring your grandmother with us and maybe just stay the night." She says.

"Okay then, looking forward to it." I tell her.

"Same here, and your dad says he loves you and he'll see you soon. And I love you too. I'm looking forward to meeting Omega and seeing Ashley too." She says.

"Yes, it will be good, and I love you too." I tell her.

"Okay, I'm going to get back to making us some dinner." She tells me.

"Okay, mom, bye." I say this before we hang up.

I'm thankful for my relationship with my mom; we have grown to respect each other.

She didn't think I could handle living on my own after April moved out.

I get ready for bed and say my goodnight prayers.

"Thank You, Father, for leading me through the day. Your presence is greatly felt. All the praise, worship, and honor go to You. Please watch over all my family and friends as we rest tonight. I love You. Amen.

I then I lay down to sleep.

CHAPTER 21
Family for One from Sunday

It's Monday morning.

My goal is to call the teacher administration and figure out my job dynamics.

I get on my knees first and foremost to say my morning prayer.

"Good morning, Heavenly Father. Thank You for waking me up this morning. Giving me Your breath, filling me with purpose for another day. Let Your will be done. Guide my steps, provide Your wisdom upon me in my job search. Provide Your wisdom for Omega and me. I want to do the right thing, Your thing. I love You. Amen."

I feel God's peace cover me after the prayer.

I check my phone and see many notifications from emails and new sources.

I see text messages from Omega.

No phone calls, so again, no returned calls from the teacher administration.

I returned the call and left a message a while ago; I can't believe I haven't gotten a call back yet.

I know they are open on Mondays, so I will call again.

I sit on my bed and call them.

"Hello, this Margret Faizer of local school teachings of America, how can I help you this morning?" A woman answers the phone.

It's the same woman, I recognize the voice.

I get nervous, and I'm not sure what to say. I know I really want to straight up ask her why she never returned my call.

"Yes, hello, good morning. My name is Sunday Suddrom. I'm calling to check on the status of my application. I also received a call from this number some time ago, and I called, left a voicemail, and have yet to hear anything." I tell her.

"Oh, yes, good morning, Miss Suddrom. We have been reviewing your application, and we are in the process of debating between you and another candidate. At this moment, I will say we are taking an interest in the other candidate; the qualifications are a bit more corresponding. If we need substitutes or a guaranteed position opens, we will call." She says.

"Ok, so that was all you were calling me about when you left that voicemail?" I ask her.

I just feel that there is more to this; I'm not sure; I'm just trying not to get upset.

"Well, yes, I'm sure that is why." She responds.

"You're sure?" I ask her confusedly.

"I go through many calls a day, Miss Suddom. If there is anything else I need, I will call you." She tells me sternly.

"I applied for the teaching job because I took classes, served the community many times, and already did the substitute work; I'm more qualified to be just a substitute." I tell her.

"I understand, and I will give you a call upon further notice. Thank you for calling." She sharply replies.

"Ok," I reply.

"Bye now." She responds before hanging up.

I look at the phone as the line beeps, signifying the call has hung up.

My heart drops, and I feel like I just ran into a wall.

My hopes were so high for this position.

I've done so much that all I wanted was to get in the door.

I want to call more and get more understanding, but I know that will only push me further back.

When has showing desperation and putting myself out there ever worked?

It surely backfired when I thought it would work with my relationship with Marcus.

I promised myself and God I would never beg; I would always come with urgency but never beg.

So, I sit back in silence, and the tears just start to roll over me.

I'm trying to hear something from God, but I know emotions are so full.

I can't help but feel rejected, denied, and lost.

Although the saying that God's rejection is His protection comes to mind, this still hurts because I have put so many good ideas into becoming a good Christian teacher.

All to represent God and His kingdom.

But, for some reason, He doesn't want that for me; maybe I misheard the mission from God; maybe it was too much of me and not enough of Him.

Now, I'm in the scene of depletion where it's too hard to hear from God because my mind is racing with thoughts, my feelings have been hurt, and it has taken so much energy out of me.

This would be a good time to eat.

Food should give me some energy.

I guess the energy needed to call around again and apply for other positions.

I still haven't replied to Omega; I just don't feel like sharing the news.

Maybe after I eat, I will work up more strength to call him.

I'll make my famous omelet and keep my mind going on eating something good.

I put my R&B Christian music on while I cooked my omelet.

I noticed more texts coming in from Omega.

My food is almost ready, and listening to the music puts me in a better mood, so I'll text him.

"Hey baby, how are you?" He asked as soon as I answered the phone.

"I'm pretty good, just making some breakfast, trying to get my day going." I briefly tell him.

"That's good; I've been texting you all morning." He tells me.

"I know, baby, I just..." And my voice starts to crack down as the thoughts of the phone call come in.

"What's wrong?" He quickly asks me.

"The teaching job is no-go. The receptionist said they found someone else, and they were considering me for the subsite position. If they needed any further information, they would call. She was so quick and rude and seemed to disqualify me." I tell him as tears roll down my face.

"Damn baby, I'm sorry. Please keep your head up, babe. I know something good is coming; you prepared hard for this, and you'll get something great for it." He says, trying to encourage me.

"I know, I just feel like I hit a roadblock and am now trying to figure out where to go next." I tell him.

"God already knows your next. He's just preparing you, and all that takes time. I know your passion and desires for teaching the kids and why that's so close to you, but you got to believe there is calling on your name somewhere, baby. I just hate to hear you cry." He tells me.

"Thanks, baby, for all the sweet, encouraging words. I'm just trying to pick myself up. I wanted to get some more applications in today and then get ready for my family to come visit on Wednesday." I tell him.

"Ok, that's great, babe, and I can't wait to meet them. Do you need anything?" He asks me.

"I'm ok for now, baby; thank you though." I tell him.

"Ok, then maybe I can see you later. I have some work to do, and I'll let you do your thing, and we can get together later." He says.

"Ok then, that sounds good." I tell him.

"Alright then, I love you." He says.

My heart leaps at his remark.

It felt good to hear that. Thank you, God.

"I love you too, baby." I say this before hanging up.

All his encouraging words filled me with comfort and motivation.

I was so nervous to tell him what I was battling with and how I felt behind.

Whenever I spoke to Marcus about things, he was always so quick to call me emotional or tell me to get over it instead of just listening to me by being an ear of support.

Somehow, it would lead to a fight, and he would tell me it's just all my fault and continue to ignore me.

Especially when it came to my struggles with college and doing the teacher assistant jobs.

He was so negative and told me it was my fault for picking something that didn't pay well and dealing with other people's children, who were probably all misbehaved.

He never saw my heart in it or understood that even though a person could love doing something, that doesn't mean the journey was going to be easy.

But Omega proved me wrong and was so supportive with his response. I held back, and I didn't want to be that type of person.

Omega is someone new; I can't compare on any level to Marcus.

Obviously, I have some reflection to do if I'm expecting past relationship to be like the current one, Omega has already shown himself worthy on so many levels.

I eat my omelet and try to really listen to the worship music playing in the background.

I spent the whole day applying for jobs and reading the news.

Most of the receptionists tell me the same thing: I need more teacher volunteering work for qualifications in that district and to apply for the substitute positions.

While searching through jobs, I came across camp and school counseling jobs.

It sparks my interest, and I have mostly all the qualifications. I got some recommendations from my church for the other skills, and I started to apply for jobs in that field.

It boosted my motivation and hope; maybe God is leading me another way.

I have wanted to come in and witness to the children about the light of God, but maybe I'm needed somewhere else—not a place I want to go, but where God wants me to go.

Omega kept to his word about coming together at the end of the day. He came with another beautiful bouquet of roses and the biggest hug.

He wanted to take me on a drive, so I put on my cute and comfortable loungewear to match his comfortable style and picked out my curls.

We drove through the city, listening to music while laughing and talking.

We went to have ramen and then ice cream for dessert.

He opened up and told me how nervous yet excited he was to meet my family and that I would be meeting his soon enough.

I'm not pushing too much on that introduction; I know they are a grieving family.

Once he got me back home with a kiss and a big hug, I thanked God for making the day beautiful.

I found the reason for my trial this morning with the job; my calling is somewhere else. I found that I have gotten a man who wants to listen to me and encourage me and is open about him needing that in return.

I found You in the storm, and I'm thankful You didn't let go of my hopeless and wretched soul.

I took a long, hot shower and washed and moisturized my hair.

I decided to read over the Psalms, starting with Chapter 1. Even when I know You, God, there is nothing like going back to reading Your word because there is always something more to the mysterious trinity.

I dozed off after reading up to chapter 12.

I'm woken by my alarm.

I get up to use the restroom and then come back to my bed and get on my knees to say my morning prayer.

"Our Father in heaven, hallowed be Your name, Your kingdom come, Your will be done, on earth as it is in heaven. Give us this day our daily bread and forgive us of our debts as we forgive our debtors, and do not lead us into temptation but deliver us from the evil one. For Yours is the kingdom, the power, and the glory forever and ever. Amen."

I get up and go back to brush my teeth and wash my face.

I check my phone to see news notifications, and I can see from the brief subject line that they are still looking for leads on the Rebecca Meyers case.

I see some emails that some of the new jobs I have applied to have been viewed, which is encouraging.

And then texts from my Omega and my mom.

My mom, dad, and grandma are coming tomorrow, and I must clean up, go to the grocery store, and make sure things are ready.

My mom always cooks when she comes, so I'll call her for ingredients to get from the store.

So mostly my job is to clean. My mom and grandma sleep together in my bed, and I get my blow-up mattress while my dad sleeps on my living room couch.

I called Omega and told him the plans for the day, and he offered to take me to the store.

I also called Ashley to remind her to come see my mom, too.

My mom and Ashley have a great relationship, and she has considered Ashley to be her third daughter since we met in college.

My mom says her journey was quite like Ashley's.

I put my gospel music on and got to cleaning my apartment. My mom loves a clean house.

Knowing her, she still finds something to clean, even when I feel the place is spotless.

But I know she'll love seeing all these rose bouquets around.

My sister called while I was cleaning.

"Have fun with mom and dad; I miss you guys; I wish I could come too." April says.

"I know I miss you, sis. I'm sorry we haven't really talked since my birthday; I just got a whole plate full of life in my hand right now." I tell her metaphorically.

"Ok, well, in between those little cracks in time, you can always call your big sis for anything." She says.

She has always been there and was the most supportive when I wanted to keep the apartment and live alone after she moved to Texas.

She helped my parents see the light in it, although they felt that moving back home and saving my inheritance was best until I found a job. She helped me convince them I couldn't be all that I learned going to college by going right back home just because things were getting tougher. I had what it takes to stand alone, and if that time ever comes, I can then go back to living with my parents.

And it was the truth, I had to take my skills and apply them.

Ideally, I wanted to stay home with my parents until a God-fearing man came, but I blinded that whole authenticity by being with Marcus all those years.

So, I'm taking the consequences from that, but I know God has turned it around to work out in my favor for His glory.

I found that when I lived alone, I could check myself, my integrity, and my morals a lot better and see that I'm planted and growing in the most important way, which is by being a better warrior for God's kingdom, which led me to start Garden Ministries.

"I will tell you about Omega as soon as I get time, April." I tell her.

I know my mom already mentioned him to her.

"Ok, good, and I'm trying not to be mad at you for not telling me first, but I know how it was when I first met Harlem; I was super hush-hush and protective." She tells me.

"But all will work well if you let God be the head of your relationship and fight for him through all the roughness." She tells me.

April and Harlem have been through a lot, but they are stronger than ever.

He really led her back to Christ when she started to make self-centered decisions and place the value of money over all else.

"Thank you, sis; I love you. I'm going to call you soon. I have to finish cleaning and then go to the store." I tell her.

"Ok, Sunday, I love you too. Bye." She says this before hanging up.

My sister has been engaged for about a year now. She said she likes the engagement stage and wants to prepare to become a great wife as much as she.

April likes to take her time with things.

Harlem and April both work really hard and love to spoil each other.

So, when they do have their wedding day, I know it will be lavishly done.

I go back to cleaning up as much as I can.

My mom then calls me.

"Hey mom, can't wait to see you guys tomorrow." I tell her excitedly.

"Me too, baby. We are getting all packed up, then I'm going to get your grandma in the morning." She tells me.

"Ok good. Is there anything you need me to get from the store?" I ask her.

"I'm still trying to decide what to cook, so we'll just go when I get there." She tells me.

"Ok, sounds good mom." I tell her.

"Alright, I love you, Sunday. I'll call you a little later. We need to get a few things done." She says.

"Ok, I love you, mom, and I'll see you soon." I tell her before hanging up.

Well, that saves me an extra trip by not having to go to the store today.

I text Omega to let him know I don't need the ride.

I'm feeling blessed as the love is all coming together as my family and friends gather soon.

Once I see that my house is spotless, I feel drained.

I know I will be having a lot of people around the next couple of days, so I decided it would be good to take a nice hot bubble bath, where I can enjoy the solemn quietness before the chaos.

I bring my speaker into the bathroom with me to play some smooth jazz. I put my gardenia-smelling bubbles in my bath, light a few candles, and sit back in the warmth.

After I get out of the bath, I clean the bathroom, put my pajamas on, and warm up a lasagna in the oven for dinner.

I enjoy the quietness; I enjoy being alone. I have had my mind space, my heart space, and my home space crowded with other people's feelings, thoughts, and attitudes.

That took a toll on me and made me put others before myself.

Now, caring for myself and cleaning out my space allows me to hear from God better so I can better help myself, which makes it a lot better for me to help others.

After I eat my lasagna and a bowl of salad, I start to feel my eyes get heavy.

I head to my room to say my night prayers before bed.

Heavenly Father, thank You for a peaceful day. I got so much done, and worshipping You all the way through made the job even better. I'm looking forward to a new day tomorrow. To a coming together, where we will give You all the honor. I love You. Thank You. Amen.

I wake up the next morning to my alarm.

I hurry to the bathroom and then come out to say my morning prayer.

Good morning, Lord. Thank You for waking me up this morning. Thank You for the breath of life, a new day to give You all the honor and praise. Please be with me and my family today. Please be with them as they travel here, and please be with us as we are joined together in unity. I love You. Amen.

I check my phone and see texts from my mom, Omega, and Ashley.

Everyone is looking forward to getting together today.

I get dressed for the day. I decided to wear a pair of jeans and a white lace T-shirt with my sparkly white slides to match.

I put my curling cream in my hair and a light layer of makeup.

I always want to look good for momma.

I head to the kitchen to make an avocado toast breakfast with a huge glass of orange juice.

I call my mom to get details of her arrival.

"Hey mom, what time will y'all be here?" I asked her as soon as she answered.

"We will get there around 2 p.m." She tells me.

"When I get there, I'll head to the store. I want to make a pot roast with rice, beans, and plantains tonight." She tells me.

Yes, Mom always throws down on the cooking.

"Ok, mom, that sounds so delicious; I can't wait." I tell her excitedly.

"How many people am I cooking for?" She asks.

I know she's asking to see if Omega will be joining. Ashley and Nick always come, so she knows to make enough for two extra people, but tonight, there will be a third extra person.

"Tonight, there will be seven of us having dinner, mom. Omega is joining us, and he's looking forward to meeting you all." I tell her.

"Ok great. We're almost done getting ready, so I'll let you know when we are near." She says.

"Ok, I love you, and drive safe," I tell her.

"Ok, I love you too. Bye." She says this before hanging up.

Sometimes, my mom lets me know when she's an hour away—30 minutes, sometimes even 10 minutes.

Then there are the occasions when she just pops up here without giving her ETA.

And today seems like a pop-up; I know she wants to see Omega.

I let Ashley know the dinner plans, and she's excited.

I called Omega to let him know, too.

"Hey baby." He sweetly says when he answers the phone.

"Hi baby, how are you?" I ask him.

"I'm doing good; I'm just finishing some things up for work. How about you, baby? How are you feeling? Are you ready to see your family?" He asks me.

"Yes, are you ready to meet them? My mom is cooking a delicious dinner tonight. So, my apartment is basically hers for the 2 days they will be here." I tell him.

"Sounds like a mom." He says it jokingly.

"Do you need me to bring anything or do anything?" He asks me.

"No, baby, just bring your sweet, handsome self. They'll be here around 2 p.m. My mom might just pop up without a call. Come whenever you're ready." I tell him.

"Ok, I'm going to come right before 2 p.m." He says.

"Ok, great, baby." I tell him.

I hear silence on the line for a second.

"That's my mom calling, babe; I know she's checking in. I'll call you back." He tells me.

"Ok, baby, no worries; take care of her. I love you; see you later." I tell him.

"I love you too." He says this before the phone call ends.

Lord, please continue to cover Omega's family; give them Your peace, Your comfort, Your joy, and Your word. I thank You for making Omega such a God-fearing man. I know he is sharing Your word with his family in times when they need to hear it, and they, too, are giving him Your encouraging words when he needs them. Thank You for still building faithful families who work from the fear of You, Lord.

Even when I just try to pray quietly in the spirit, it comes out, and I'm in tears, feeling the peace of God.

I know He will answer prayers.

A couple of hours pass by, and I get a text from Omega saying that he is 10 minutes away.

I soon heard him knocking on the door.

I opened it to see him holding three bouquets of flowers. I didn't even have room to go in for a hug.

"For you, your mom and grandma." He tells me.

I grab them from him and place them on the counter to be arranged.

"Wow, baby, thank you; these are all so beautiful. They're going to love them too." I tell him

I was finally greeted with a big hug and a warm kiss from him after we put down all the flowers.

"How did everything go with your mom?" I ask him as we make our way to my living room couch.

"She's doing ok; she was going to take a trip to Tennessee soon to visit some family. I told her about you and the plans to meet your family today. She said hi, and she would like to meet you as well. She's just getting herself together. The investigator called and said they have some type of lead that the person who hit Maximum was a female suspect." He tells me.

My heart drops at the thought. A woman may have done this.

"Wow, this is crazy." I tell him.

"Yeah, they said they would be over to my parents' house later or tomorrow morning to present to them the findings." He says.

"At this point, my mom just wants to find peace and be out of the city; she believes whoever did this is already suffering enough and clearly was suffering before to have done this." He continues to say.

"Yes, your mom is so strong; I can't wait to meet her, and I know Tennessee is beautiful." I tell him.

"Yeah, it's nice, perfect for everything homegrown, for quietness, for nature, and to be off the grid." He says.

"I'm praying that peace finds your family, and whatever news the investigator brings will only encourage everyone." I tell him as I lean in to hug and kiss him.

I hear my doorbell ring, and I know that's mom and family.

Of course, she was going to show up without an ETA.

"They're here." I say as we get up to go to the door.

I open the door, and I'm greeted with love from my mom, dad, and grandmother.

Omega introduces himself, and everyone is hugging.

My nerves settle at that comfort.

My mom, grandma, and I gather in the kitchen to see all the ingredients we need for dinner.

My dad and Omega make themselves comfortable on the couch, scrolling through channels looking for a game.

I can see them engaging in conversation, and it seems to be going well.

When my mom and grandma decided that they were ready to go to the store, I realized Omega would be here alone with my dad.

I go over and tell Omega that we will be leaving to see what he intends to do.

"Ok, gentlemen, us ladies are headed to the store to pick up a couple of things? Are y'all good? Do you need anything?" I looked, asking them both.

"No, I'm good, sweetheart; I'll just sit here with your pops and find some games." Omega says.

"Yes, we're good, baby girl. Tell your mom not to forget my pie." He says this while laughing.

Ok, Lord, continue to let them get along.

"You want to use my car for trunk space?" He asks me while handing me the keys.

"Yes, thank you, baby." I say this while grabbing the keys.

All the family stands around, looking impressed.

I've never driven his truck before; I like being the passenger, but I'm excited to give it a drive.

My mom, grandma, and I head down to my parking garage and get into the truck.

"Wow, look at this big, beautiful truck; he got it going on Sunday." My grandma says while being so impressed.

Grandma has always encouraged April and me to find good, godly men who have firm bank accounts, too.

"Thank you, granny." I say while giggling.

"Yes, this is nice." My mom says this while looking around.

"You have to tell me more about him Sunday." My mom says.

"I know mom, but I want him to be the one to tell you more about himself." I tell her.

The drive to the store was about 10 minutes, and we talked about Omega the whole time.

My grandma and mom liked everything that they heard about him.

It feels good to have family interest, but I already knew they would like him.

Once at the store, my mom, grandma, and I shopped around for all we needed and had a good time catching up.

We were there longer than planned; luckily, we left appetizers and snacks out for my dad and Omega.

We get back to my apartment, and my dad and Omega are watching a boxing match and deep into the commentary.

We let them know about the groceries in the truck, and they headed down to get the bags out of the trunk.

I'm so glad to see everyone getting along. I feel the peace of God in my place.

After I prep the food, I sneak off and head to my room while my grandma and mom begin to cook.

I get on my knees to pray.

Heavenly Father, thank You for letting love win and bringing family together for joy, laughter, and good food. We are stronger together and better with You at the center, and I feel You in this place. Thank You for being the Lord of my life. Amen.

I hear Ashley and Nick in the living room; they have arrived, filling the house with more love and laughter.

The night continued with a good meal and games we all played together.

As my family got ready for bed, Omega, Nick, Ashley, and I sat and talked a little while longer on my balcony.

After Nick and Ashley left and I kissed Omega goodbye, I made sure my dad was comfortable on the pull-out couch in the living room and headed to my room with my mom and grandma.

We laid up and talked for some more time, and they shared how much they like Omega and are looking forward to seeing more of him.

I opened up more about my battle with getting a teaching job and how the receptionist talked to me.

They gave me words of encouragement, and we read over Bible scriptures about His plans and how trials show our dependence on God, which He wants, and how, in the end, all the tarrying on will fit perfectly in His time.

We all prayed together and then went to bed.

My family stayed another night, and we all came back together, filling my little apartment up.

Enjoying life and the present time.

Omega and I have grown and developed a foundation together since my parents left, leading to a stronger relationship.

We read the Bible together, pray together, encourage each other, share our dreams, and remain honest with one another, with the main quality being love.

Time has flown by, and it feels like I've known him all this lifetime.

I'm most grateful for both the ups and downs.

I feel us becoming one.

CHAPTER 22
Mega Family and Beyond

Omega and I have been able to be a blessing to others, especially those in a hunger crisis.

We have donated and curated many food drives and expanded food businesses.

To see him so open and filled with joy, helping those within the community and the church has inspired me and shows that God is working through him.

Garden Ministries and Mega Eating have collaborated with many of the restaurants that Omega does food critiquing.

Every week, we have 2-3 food drives.

We have hopes of becoming global.

Nick and Ashley have used their car services to help get those in need to shelters, job interviews, and church free of charge.

We have expanded our businesses together and have individually deepened our dependence on God.

Omega and I went to Santa Barbara and stayed at a beautiful hotel, we managed well with separate beds.

This was our official first trip together.

We stayed for the weekend and met some more vendors to donate to his organization.

I also had a spa day and was able to gift another woman a spa day experience.

I selected this woman out of a crowd while eating, and the Holy Spirit directed me to her.

He also wined and dined me with a night full of romance and laughter.

There is no doubt about the love being there; it is the love of God we both share, knowing how much God loves us individually and the great love He puts between us.

Omega and I have fallen in love and are patient with each other.

We've been holding on to the information from Rebecca Meyer's case and taking it to God daily about what we should do.

I've been able to push the idea of Cain to the back of my head and what he did with and to Rebecca.

It's still a very active case, even though it has been almost six months, and other breaking news stories have arisen.

It's good to know that the media did give Rebecca a lot of attention. Usually when a black woman goes missing it doesn't get the same play as when a white woman goes missing.

I just battle with knowing I may play an active part in the case by holding the information I now know.

I know the longer this goes on, the more people will start to paint the image of Rebecca as a disgraceful woman who shouldn't have been running the streets, and this is what she gets.

Since being back home and settled from our trip, I got some cleaning done around the house and more organizing.

I checked my mail in the lobby and saw a letter from the teacher's administration and two letters from the counseling companies I applied to.

I say a quick prayer to God as I walk back to my apartment and begin to open the letter with a spark of excitement and fear.

The teacher's administration offered me a part-time position in New Orleans.

My heart dropped; I couldn't believe that this was where they placed me.

I feel a wave of confusion as my aspirations of becoming a teacher arise, but it's not where or how I expected it.

I wanted to get established in this career in California at a Christian-based elementary school.

I looked up the school the administration assigned me to, and that school didn't seem to be faith-based.

Maybe this school needed a touch of guidance, and that's where I was hoping to have the help of Garden Ministries, but New Orleans is too far for that.

I couldn't manage to move to New Orleans alone. Then, try to expand or make Garden Ministries virtual. Then apply the new curriculum to students whose parents may not have applied Christ to their lives.

I was expecting to go where faith was already established, not having to start a new, especially alone. Even though I started Garden Ministries, I had my girls with me.

I especially couldn't do all of this as a part-time facilitator.

I wasn't expecting the highest pay, but that pay grade could equate to a nice apartment in Louisiana.

This offer doesn't settle with me, but it's all I got.

My thriving relationship with Omega is here in California, and I see progress in that.

It's beyond just seeing potential; he shows me his growth and virtue daily.

I opened the letters from the counseling companies.

One offer is for a traveling counselor through high schools in Southern California.

The other job is a school counselor for transitioning students, some from foster care, some graduates, and some who are learning to manage coming to a new school.

It's located in the next district over.

The letter also goes on to say that I will need to complete a couple more courses on counseling to get a license.

That offer is much better than the first; I've managed to keep a great portion of my inheritance in an investment account and the rest I use for rent and living.

So, paying for classes will set back my finances.

All I can do is give these options to God because it's a lot for me to juggle and debate over.

I put the letters in my prayer closet.

I grab my phone to call Ashley to discuss 'Man can with God' service.

Omega and Nick are both preparing their testimonies with a couple of other men at the church.

I know Omega has been putting a lot of effort into what he's going to say.

I can tell he's been kind of anxious about it, but I've been encouraging him and telling him to trust that the Holy Spirit will interfere on his behalf.

"Hey Sunny girl, what are you doing?" Ashley asks when she answers the phone.

"I'm just cleaning up some things around the house. I haven't unpacked all my luggage; I'm ready to go back to Santa Barabra." I tell her.

"Girl, I bet it was so beautiful. I'm so glad y'all went together." She says.

"Everything was nice, even the long drive." I tell her while I start reminiscing about the beautiful weather, the food, and the good experience with Omega.

"I know it was girl, and you have to show me pictures of everything." She tells me.

"I will. April is putting together all the pictures in a scrapbook for us. You know she loves doing that." I tell Ashley.

"That's so sweet; I can't wait for it. So, when do you think she'll meet him?" Ashley asks.

"Hopefully soon; he loves traveling, so if she's not able to come here, we will go there." I tell her.

I get excited thinking about another trip with Omega. Whether we drive or fly to Texas, I know it will be such a fun time.

He's so good and persistent about enjoying details, big or small, about life.

"I know April is already so fond of him; my mom has talked him up so much." I continue to say.

I love and appreciate the family support; they have been so great with Omega.

My mom always checks in on both of us and prays for us.

"That's good, girl; God is leading the way. Did she tell you about any wedding plans for her and Harlem yet?" She asks me.

"Yes, she said they are coming up with an official save the date now. My mom is so annoyed with their delays. But they're happy with the time they are taking. We've learned from the past that continuing to ask April 'when she was going to get married', would just make her go ghost on us; she said she doesn't like feeling under pressure." I tell her.

"I can't blame her. Let it be their time, their happiness, and their way with God, of course. I know my parents hit me with that 'when' too." She tells me.

"So, when will Nick propose?" I jokingly ask her in a mother-like tone.

We both started laughing.

"I love him too much to put time restraints on it now, but I have faith to know it's coming soon." She says it confidently.

"That's good, sis, and I know he will very soon in the most beautiful way too." I tell her.

"Thank you." She says this, pretending to cry.

"And I know Omega is destined to make you his wife soon." She tells me.

I have confidence in that, too.

"God's will, and I won't accept anything less." I say to her.

"Speaking of, how is his testimony going for service?" I ask her.

"Good, he's almost done, but I should also go check on him, he's locked himself away trying to concentrate." She tells me.

"What a duty." I say this as we both laugh.

"Ok, I love you, girl. Talk to you soon." She says.

"Ok, I love you. Bye." I say this before hanging up.

I sit back and thank God after talking to Ashley. Our friendship is one of the most important relationships in my life.

We have grown together in our faith and supported one another by picking each other up when we get lost in the world and even when the world is at our feet.

I know Omega was having a hard time putting his testimony together.

With the loss of his young brother and his family being long distant, he's been lonely. Also battling with struggles that come with grief and the investigation of his brother, he, at times, feels helpless.

But he has put down the drinking habit and turned his life around.

When he does talk to his parents, they are so proud to hear about him recovering from his drinking habit and his new relationship with me.

But on top of the loss and battle, he's carrying the weight of the information about Rebecca Meyers.

We have kept this between us, praying about it and trying to find a way through it with God.

We both know that holding such information isn't fair to anyone, especially both of us, due to the weight it carries.

It's coming closer to the realization and truth that God brought us together, but all good things come with a sacrifice.

And we both know that sacrifice is coming soon, and that's what will bring justice.

We are not our own, so when we don't reflect holy behavior, we aren't being the image of Him that God created us to be.

Omega and I are both coming to terms with it while sustaining love.

I decided to give him more time to get through his day and get to his testimony.

I go to my desk in my room and organize my work and new job offers.

This week, leading up to the 'Man Can with God' service, I will devote myself to making an official work decision.

So many things to consider, all risking being further away from Omega.

I don't want to stress him with my work decisions while he's trying to prepare his testimony and manage the new food truck vendors that are coming to town.

He will be critiquing food, writing and managing blogs, speaking with the food truck owners, and then serving food for those in need through his organization.

I'm here as his helping hand.

I'm grateful we had a nice vacation before he hurried back to work.

As the past three days went on, Omega and I had quick conversations over the phone.

He's been preparing for work and writing his testimony.

I've been organizing some things for Garden Ministries.

And so, we made plans to have a date night so we could take a break from work and enjoy some personal time.

Tonight is date night.

And I'm dressed in a little red body-fitting dress.

My curls are big, bright, and bouncy, just the way Omega likes them.

I add a light layer of makeup, and as I'm applying my lip gloss, I get a text from Omega saying that he will be here in 10 minutes.

I take a small leap for excitement; I can't wait to be in his arms.

I clean up the small mess I made and head to the living room to put my shoes on, which match my dress.

The TV was on the news station, and I saw Rebeca Meyer's mother speaking to the media, asking for information about her daughter.

She's crying out for Rebecca to come home, but she has also accepted that she may never and would like even the smallest amount of information to settle her soul.

My throat begins to choke up.

Omega and I have felt the burden of knowing Cain is the prime suspect in this case.

We don't want to lose remorse.

Nothing can release the weight it carries.

And I know that as the days go on and no one else comes to release information, it lands on Omega and me to speak up.

The doorbell rings, bringing me out of my thoughts.

I go to answer the door to see Omega standing so handsomely, wearing an all-white shirt and a light blue pair of jeans with design marks on them.

He's also wearing white loafers that match his attire.

All while carrying a big, beautiful bouquet of red roses.

"Hey, beautiful woman." He says this while greeting me, hugging me with one arm as he holds the roses with his other hand.

"Hi baby, I've missed you. I'm so glad to see you." I say this to him as I let go of the hugging embrace and grab the roses.

"Same here, baby; I've been looking forward to this all day." He says this as he comes in behind me.

He arranged for us to have a seafood dinner near the coast after meeting with some new restaurant owners earlier this week.

He pulls me in for another hug, and this time, he grabs my chin for a kiss.

We are passionate about our moment with gazing eyes. As we released from hugging, I hear more about Rebecca being talked of on the news.

Rebecca's mother isn't giving her speech anymore, but a news anchor is talking about her family and how lost and saddened they are, with no leads.

Omega and I both look at each other.

"It's becoming hard to say what the right thing is to do." He says this as he takes a seat on my counter stool.

"Yeah, I know, this has all been pretty heavy." I say to him.

"I haven't stopped praying about it and asking God to lead me to do the right thing." He says.

"That's good, baby, and I'm here for you either way." I tell him while touching him assuredly.

"I think we both know what the right thing to do is; it's just trusting God to guide us there." He says.

"Yes, baby, I know." I tell him.

He then stands up for another hug.

We haven't been holding this information on our own; God is sustaining us.

With all the little crises going on in our individual lives, there is no way we could sustain ourselves without God.

Now it's time for God's timing of when to say something.

He's been developing us in the meantime.

Omega grabs my hand as we walk out the door and head to his car.

The drive there was peaceful. Driving along the coast is one of our favorite things to do together, and it's even better when we're going to have dinner somewhere.

Once we arrived and were seated and welcomed by the owner and some of the other workers who were looking forward to meeting Omega, we were served amazing house specials, including appetizers and entrees.

We smiled, laughed, and enjoyed the whole evening.

Afterward, as we were all full, we walked near the water.

The warm breeze is refreshing and relaxing.

"My parents are coming into town on Sunday," Omega says as we slowly stroll.

I know that's probably what could've been stressing Omega out more.

"That's great, babe. I know you're looking forward to seeing them." I tell him.

"Yeah, and for you to meet them, they would like to have dinner Sunday when they get in. I told them our Sundays are church, lunch, and relaxing." He says.

"Plus, we have our 'Men can with God' service and all." He continues.

I can tell by the way he said that, that he's been having a hard time writing it out.

"How's your testimony going?" I ask him.

"I'm at the end of what I want to say but it was a struggle to write it all out." He says.

"Great, babe, we are looking forward to it. Will your parents be in by Sunday before church?" I ask him.

"No later that evening; that's why they said dinner would be the best time." He says.

"Ok, baby, church, then dinner later with your family for Sunday." I say to him.

"Alright. They'll be here for about 3 days, checking on some property and meeting with the detective for Maximum." He says.

"Wow, is there more information for them?" I ask him.

"They said it might just be a small piece of information, but anything is worth talking through." He says.

"Ok, that sounds good; we'll get through this with them and with prayer." I tell him.

"Thanks babe." He says this, bringing me closer to him.

We head back to the car after laughing some more about all that we see.

Our drive-back was nice, with some low music playing in the back.

Omega holds my hand and gives it kisses and rubs during the ride.

Once he walks me up to my apartment and kisses me goodnight, I head to my room to wash my face, shower, and put my pajamas on.

When I get out of the shower, Omega calls to say I love you and goodnight.

I then get on my knees to say a prayer.

Heavenly Father, thank You for all that You are doing in the lives of Your children. You aren't forgetting us. You're bringing peace and justice while setting us free. That's why You are the God of all things, the King of the universe. We can't do this with our strength. Please protect and bring peace to my family, Omega's family, and all our friends. Please help Omega continue to fight the good fight of faith in Your honor for Your glory, and help us all, including myself, as we try so desperately to get closer to Your heart. Thank You for leading us with the gift of the Holy Spirit. I love You. Amen.

The next couple of days have gone by quickly.

Omega finished some deals with restaurants.

Nick and Ashley have spread the driving business to another city in California.

My parents won a trip on a cruise ship.

Garden Ministries has extended hours as members and new members needed places to come and eat and relax.

I also bought Omega some cologne to celebrate his day.

I have begun to write letters about the job offers I have received, but I'm still debating my choices.

Today is Sunday, and we will be honoring God and the men of the church with the 'Man can with God' service.

Plus, I'm meeting Omega's family for the first time.

I'm filled with nerves and excitement.

Omega will be picking me up for church, and I'm almost done getting ready.

I decide to wear my turquoise dress with a big bow on the back.

I have white heels to wear with it, and I'll have my curls in a half-up, half-down style.

I spray some of my best perfume.

Omega said he'd be here soon.

As I finish up the touches of makeup, I hear his knock on the door.

I greet him with a huge hug and then hand him his gift.

"Wow, thank you, babe. Can I open it now?" He asks so sweetly.

"Yes," I say.

He goes into the bag, takes the gift paper out, and is happy to see the YSL cologne.

Omega has a great cologne collection, and he always smells so amazing.

I knew he would appreciate the new edition, and I wanted to let him know how proud I am of him and that he's greatly appreciated.

"Thanks, baby; this smells so good. Thank you; this really means a lot." He says it with love.

"You're welcome, babe; we have a big day, and I just wanted you to know I'm all here for you." I tell him.

He takes me in for a big hug.

"You look beautiful too; I'll be looking right out at you when I'm up there speaking." He says.

"I'll be right there." I tell him while I give him a kiss.

I grab the rest of my things and lock the door before we head to the church.

We'll make it just in time for Bible study, which is being led by Ashley this morning.

On the drive to church, we enjoyed some gospel music that got our spirits going.

We make it to church and find a parking spot right on time.

Everyone is excited to see one another and for the 'Man can with God' service following Bible study.

Ashley's facilitation was great during Bible study; she had games to play and handed out uniquely designed daily bread that fit the story of Simon turning into Peter.

Simon was renamed Peter for his faith in Jesus; he became Jesus's right-hand man, leading him to become a fisher of men, not just a fisherman anymore.

And Peter is one we can relate to due to his passion and his struggles when he denied Jesus three times.

Peter was a great man to speak about today for the 'Man can with God' service.'

After the Pastor gave a great sermon on King David, the congregation all shouted and praised the Lord, and we began the 'Man can with God' segment.

Nick and all the other men who were in the program to speak gave such touching testimonies that moved everyone's heart.

Their love and walk for Christ show how God can turn ashes into beauty.

Ashley and Nick held each other after he spoke, and he really opened up about his journey like never before.

Omega was the last to speak, and I gave him a hug before walking up to the podium in the pulpit.

"Hello, my amazing church family. I want us to give all glory to God for what He has done for the men in this house. I know the woman here has been affected by this, too. Thank you, my brothers, in Christ, for remaining great examples for this generation and generations to come. Thank you for helping me get the strength to get up here, too. I thank You, Holy Spirit, for Your presence. His presence never left me; even while growing up as an only child, I got lonely. My parents worked hard creating computer systems, making a good life for us, and a lot of those times I was left alone but I was then showered with gifts. I accepted them as a child, of course, because what kid doesn't want toys? But I also thought that maybe my parents didn't want more kids because they didn't like me, not wanting to create another me. I was very loud as a child; talking back was the least of it. I wanted so badly to control myself. I wanted to make my own name; I wanted to go where I wanted to when I wanted. I thought I learned a lot from being an only child, cooking, and maintaining myself when my parents weren't home. So, I thought I knew it all. I became resentful in a spoiled, ungrateful way. I was acting out because I just wanted to be held. My parents did the best they could, which caused them to be work addicts because they were running from their own poverty-driven demons. And I started to understand this after finding a study guide in the book of Job. I was at the library looking for job skill sets, and I thought Job from the Bible said job. And I read it, and I realized that I was never alone. That God was always there, and he put me and my family through our trials and tribulations because there was something bigger than us that needed to be exposed, more to give Him glory, and He knew that once we found Him, we would never let Him go. I was locked in and anchored after reading that Bible study guide, which I never returned. I talked to my mom more about it; she was easier to talk with about things, and she explained that she knew I would come to this eventually; that's why she never feared for my safety. And how often God told her I was her chosen child, she didn't need another, and that I would make a difference. I would just have to learn what all of this was about first. I felt honored; I felt that I found myself from within. But I also felt the weight and the pressure, and no matter how many times I read Job, I still fought with God for allowing the hard times, forgetting the why. When my mom found out she was pregnant again with a boy, I was 20 and thought the whole chosen child statement went out the window. As soon as that became apparent, I started to drink more, which became another tactic the devil used to throw me off. My love for food and critiquing came about because eating a lot would sober me up the quickest. I used that to hide my flaw, but God still used me to create a way to help His people not go hungry; I still didn't see it yet. But I found that within my little brother, Maximum, he was the wisest, most mature boy, and that seemed to be unreal sometimes like he was an angel. I'm tearing up because he tragically passed away just some time ago. And it changed me even more because I know how good God is to remind me of His grace and purpose in my life through my little brother, whom I know He blessed us with because we all kept falling short and we needed a reminder that, as God's chosen to keep fighting, things will get taken from you, but you will see God the most in those storms. I know that's why my family's grievance is shown through gratitude, forgiveness, and love. So, I was shown the light again, and I stopped drinking when he showed me a beautiful soul, Garden Ministries' very own Sunday Suddrom. Since then, I have prayed more, loved more, given more, and talked to God like the best friend or father He really is. Even now, as I feel that I'm juggling and holding something dark in me, God is guiding my way to redemption and justice. Even saying that out loud is a battle because I, like Peter, come to my doubts and feel that when that time comes, I will deny Him due to fear. But God has already shown me loss, redemption, and forgiveness in my life, and I know He won't stop now. So once again and forever, as He puts breath in my lungs, I thank Him, and I thank you, church, for listening. God bless.

Everyone starts clapping and standing for Omega as he leaves the podium and comes back to sit next to me.

Omega went so deep, sharing such passion and truth.

His story was so touching and humbling; the way he spoke of his parents and little brother brought love and honor to them.

I know he really put his heart into it.

And I know what he was referring to about the dark thing he's holding inside; I know it's been a battle for him.

I don't want to get into that topic by asking him specifically about what he plans to do now, knowing that justice needs to be served.

But it's pleasing to know he's being moved by God to do something about it.

After we gathered and talked, the Pastor thanked the men and all who participated. We then headed to the car.

We let Ashley and Nick know we would be joining Omega's family a little later for dinner, so we would skip having a big lunch with them at our usual spot.

Ashley is so glad that I'm meeting his parents.

Omega and I decide to hang out at his house until his parents arrive.

I really liked the dress I wore to church and feel that it would be great for dinner, too, so there's no need to go home and change.

Omega and I talked about how great service was; we talked about food as we snacked, and I told him how proud I was of him.

His parents were giving us updates on how soon they'd be here as we waited.

We played a couple of board games until we heard the doorbell ring.

His parents were here.

I stand up to straighten out my dress as Omega walks to the front door to let them in.

I feel the waves of nerves come over me. I just want to say the right thing.

I figured that I would let them lead the conversations and questions.

I hear them being so happy to see Omega. I sit back in the living room so they can have their time together.

They enter the living room, and Omega comes to stand next to me as he officially introduces us.

They greeted me with warm smiles and hugs.

As the evening went on, my nerves loosened. Omega's mom, Carmen, and I talked through the car ride to the restaurant and on the way back to Omega's home.

She really is the sweetest woman, and she made me feel so comfortable and loved.

We talked about God, church, Omega, family, work, and scripture, and she slightly opened up about Maximum.

Omega and his dad, David, engaged with us here and there, but they were mostly tuned into their own conversations.

I'm so glad that all went well with his family. I see where he gets his charm, characteristics, and gentleness from.

I think back on his testimony from church earlier and see that he has always known he's had great parents; he just appreciates them now as he understands his position in the kingdom.

Carmen gave me such encouraging words for my job search. I didn't mention the offers I had because I would want to talk with Omega about them first.

She was pleased with the ministry I created with Ashley and is so glad about the outreach we incorporated and how Mega Eats is involved.

She was mostly proud to hear Omega's constant drinking had stopped.

The night was getting late, but we were all enjoying relaxing and talking together.

His parents were staying with him in his guest room, which he prepared for them throughout the week.

Carmen said she wanted to say a prayer before she and David went to bed, and Omega would take me home.

"Our gracious King, thank You for bringing us together as a family this evening. Your love and way conquer all. I pray that you keep us close as you watch over us. Thank you for continuing to bring health and wellness to this family. Please allow the day with the detective tomorrow to be one of justice and peace. Thank You for abundance. In Your heavenly name, we pray, Amen."

They will meet tomorrow to discuss new evidence for Maximum's case.

We all hug goodnight, and Omega then drives me home.

We had quite a peaceful drive, plus I know we are both tired from the day.

Once he walks me to my front door, he pulls me in for a big hug and kiss.

"Thank you, Sunday. I love you." He says it so gently.

I felt myself fall in love ten times over.

"Yes, baby, I love you too." I say this to him as I pull in for another kiss.

"I'll call you soon." He says this as he walks away.

I get to my room, clean up, and shower for bed.

Omega called one last time to say goodnight.

And I get on my knees to say a prayer.

"Thank You, Christ Jesus, for such a beautiful day. Thank You for Your presence, for never leaving, and for bringing us all closer together. I love You, Amen."

CHAPTER 23
We Came Too Far to Just Come This Far

After the weekend with his parents' visit had passed, Omega and I had gone back to work for his organization and the ministry.

The service for 'Man Can With God' went viral, and business for Omega and Nick accelerated.

People were happy that God-fearing men were establishing and running these businesses.

It has also been a blessing for the church, with many new members and people looking to be saved and baptized.

We've established prayer circles where members or even the church board can come for prayers.

We've been able to reach within the ministry to serve food to the community, schools, and members.

The pastor has been able to start a program to help young men coming in after graduating from school to train to be pastors.

Omega and I have kept our foundation firm and flowing with God as our source.

We have overcome many obstacles to manage the business, church, and money.

Making a great team and helping God's people.

We haven't gotten around to talking more about Rebecca Meyer's case; it's been almost three weeks since we mentioned it.

We have stayed away from news circulation, focusing on what's needed at the church.

I still haven't told Omega about my job offers and how they may require me to move.

I emailed the companies back to let them know I would get back to them with a definite answer after weighing my options and talking to Omega.

Within all the business, Omega and I made sure to make time for the two of us with date nights, movie nights, and what we call spontaneous nights, where we would take a drive wherever the Holy Spirit leads us and what captures us, we'll do.

There have been activities such as clay sculpture classes, the zoo, and even a street clean-up event.

It has made me fall in love with him even more, seeing how he always wants to help people with nothing in return.

He's always so humble and consistent in all he does.

I trust him with my life and can see him as a great husband and father, leading his family as Christ.

We open up and share our flaws with each other, which has helped us pick each other up when needed.

We are going on a date tonight, which is also the grand opening of a new authentic taco place.

Omega sometimes feels bad that work and date night blend, but it's usually always fun, and we have as good of a time as usual.

I'm looking forward to seeing him work.

I'm dressed in a silky purple dress that I know Omega loves to see me in.

And my cute glittery sandals that match the dress.

He calls to let me know he's on his way as I finish my hair and makeup.

I'm just finishing my final touches when he knocks on the door.

I open the door, and I'm greeted by him and a bouquet of white roses.

I hug and kiss him so deeply.

"Thank you, baby, these are beautiful; they smell so good." I tell him with gratitude.

"You're welcome, and you look beautiful; you know that dress always gets me going." He says it with a giggle.

I do a cute spin for him, then walk to place the bouquet on my coffee table.

"My florist sold me on the white roses today, and I could smell how freshly picked they are." He tells me.

"Wow, babe, he builds the best bouquets; he really knows his work." I say to him.

He has been faithfully getting my roses and flowers for our moms and for the church for different events at 'Maurice's Wonderful Flowers.'

"Ya, that's my guy. How are you, baby? Are you ready?" Omega asks me.

"I'm good; happy to see you, and I'm ready to go," I tell him as I grab my keys and lock the door behind me. We head down to his car.

The drive is about 45 minutes into the city of Los Angeles.

We arrive, and we see the line of people for the grand opening.

People of all backgrounds and ethnicities all want to eat some good tacos.

I also see the news media and journalists preparing to speak to the owner.

Omega parks in the back designated parking area.

He walks over to open the door for me as I'm applying my lip gloss, and we walk hand in hand to the front of the restaurant.

The crowd of people notice Omega and are always so excited to see him.

It's always amazing to see how people react to him and how he's so kind in return.

As the grand opening event goes on, it's so good to see people peacefully socializing, taking pictures, and loving the food.

I'm talking with people and having a great time telling them about the church and ministry, something Omega and I establish at any critiquing event with large masses of people.

And it's always great to see the turnout come that Sunday.

When Omega and I finally sit down to eat food after the crowd starts to ease down, the owner comes over to thank him for all his support.

And he gracefully gave a donation to the church and ministry.

We had been eating all day, but we ordered some food to go, sat back, and waited for it.

People who were still arriving came up and said hi to Omega, and some asked for a picture.

Then, out of nowhere, a white woman with long blonde hair and a purple two-piece matching outfit set comes up to our table. She stood out more than any other person who approached us, and I felt a lot of force come with her.

"Hey Omega." She says it in a seductive tone.

He looks, and I can tell he recognizes her, but he doesn't match her reply.

"Hey." He says it with a short response.

I continue to look at him, trying to read his face.

"I know you remember me and us. How are you?" She continues to ask in that tone.

"I'm doing fine, thanks." He's keeping his head down now.

And it seems like neither one of them notices I'm there, or at least she's pretending I'm not, and he's trying to avoid this whole confrontation altogether.

"Do you remember me? I came to see you at this event. To see how big you're getting." She says.

"Yeah, I know you, and thanks for coming." He replies shortly.

"Okay, so I don't get a warmer welcome; maybe a hug; can I sit and talk with you for a minute?" She asks.

"I'm here with my girl, but thanks for coming to support the new place." He says this while shaking his head.

"Oh, Omega, you're silly; you act like I don't see her, but I'm talking to you." She says this while getting closer to him.

I'm just sitting back to see how he handles this.

"Yeah, Kelsey, I see you, and like I said, I'm here with my woman, and I'm not interested in sitting and talking with you." He says it sternly.

Yeah, Kelsey, I say in my head.

"Really, Omega, all that history for nothing." She says as she puts her hands on her hips with an attitude.

One more crazy remark from her, and I'll be stepping in to say something.

I'm trying to give Omega his space to handle whatever this is, but I'm beginning to get uncomfortable, especially knowing what his past consists of.

"Kelsey, you know we've been done and left that at that. Why are you pushing on me up here?" He stands up to say it in her face.

"Omega, I supported you and always knew you would become these great things. I know you said you felt like you weren't deserving, but I'm sorry for not appreciating all of that now." She says to him.

"Okay, Kelsey, you're going to have to find something else to do; you need to step away from here, disrespecting me and my man." I firmly tell her as I stand up.

"He can speak for himself, and I was in his life before you came in; I know him very well. So this is barely disrespectful." She says to me.

"Well, can't you see that neither one of us cares?" I tell her quickly.

"You should only be here for the grand opening because there is nothing here for us." He says as he grabs my hand, and we begin to walk away.

"No, love Omega, like we didn't go through a lot together." She shouts.

I really hope she doesn't cause a scene.

"Yeah, that was then, and you know it wasn't going to last, so this is me now." Omega says as he looks at me.

"Ya sure, whatever; I just know you were loving on me last time we were together." She says.

"Right Kelsey, a long time ago, get out of the past." He says as he holds my hand while we walk away.

We go to the front and ask the server if our takeout is ready, and he walks back to check.

I can tell by the look on his face that he's upset with what just happened.

I look back and see Kelsey walking away.

He's never mentioned her, but from the conversation, I guess that was the last girl he was with.

We have had some cases when women try to push up on Omega or make forward remarks even when I'm there, but no ex.

The past and the women that were there never really get to me; I know my man is handsome, and I know that he's here with and for me now.

But this Kelsey experience was different, not so settling.

The server hands us our to-go order and thanks Omega again for coming and supporting the grand opening.

He kindly smiles and grabs my hand as we walk to his car.

The walk to the car is quiet, and when we arrive, he opens the car door for me.

He gets in on the driver's side, starts the engine, and then leans his head back with a huge exhale.

"Sorry about all of that." He says while remaining still.

"Is everything okay?" I ask him.

I'm not sure how he's feeling or thinking.

I know I'm a bit bothered and feel that this woman could cause some strife by the way he's reacting and because the devil will use anybody.

"It's all good. I know I've never mentioned her, but she was the last person I was with before I met you. And there was too much drama there." He says.

I wonder if she was around when Omega last saw Rebecca with Cain.

I don't want to get into that now; I'm just leaving the space open so he can share what this is.

"Okay, that was a bit tense, and you seem upset." I tell him.

"Well yeah, I am. She's trying to play victim to the situation, and of course it happens at an event." He says.

"What do you mean, of course?" I ask him.

Was he expecting or waiting for her to pop up again?

"She saw my career and business rising with this and was very adamant about sabotaging it because I separated from her. I knew we weren't ever going to be serious; she loved drinking and all the things I was trying to get away from—too much." He goes on to say.

Sabotage!

"Well, what does she want? What is she expecting from you?" I quickly asked him.

We are potentially facing the storm of another woman.

"Probably to try to come back in because she knew my weakness and what I was fighting with when I started to drink too much." He says.

"When was the last time you saw her? Does she know that's not you anymore and that you really don't want to be with her?" I ask him.

"It was over 2 months ago, and yes, I told her. I made it clear that I don't date around and have girlfriends; I want a wife. And I knew who the candidates for that position were, and based on that, I would give in return my true commitment. Kelsey didn't get that, and made up her own idea of us in her head." He tells me.

I sat in silence, taking this all in.

Thoughts instantly enter my head of this past, the old Omega.

This man was sexually active at one point, and I just looked the woman he was active in the eyes.

I can only imagine what that relationship entailed at that time; he was active with all those past transgressions in his life. And he was also able to manage to start a big business, and Kelsey was there to see it all. And she even said she knew he would always be great. That may not have been his girlfriend, but she experienced a lot of marks in his life.

"She didn't seem to care about me standing there." I manage to say.

"That's how she is. She always inserts herself in other people's business and jumps in when she wants to." He said it in an annoyed tone.

"Well, if that's something you don't like, why were you with her?" I ask him shyly.

I honestly held back from saying that.

I didn't want to come off with low self-esteem, but I honestly wanted to know. She was completely rude.

"I was living a different lifestyle. Doing drugs and drinking doesn't give you a clear mind. There's no anchor. I was floating along, and she just inserted herself into my life, adding more of those issues." He tells me.

I'm still not settled, and I don't feel she will give up her feelings.

"I guess, maybe we should get going now." I tell him.

"What do you mean, you guess?" He looks at me sharply.

"I mean, we haven't had any problems before, and now things are coming to the surface," I say to him quickly.

"She isn't a problem; she isn't going to do anything after I removed myself with you there." He explains.

"You just said she inserts herself and gets into people's business." I tell him

"It's cool, alright! Everything is going to be straight; I've taken care of it." He says.

I can't help but have all these thoughts in my mind. I know our thoughts aren't our own, but the swarm of these thoughts is beginning to overwhelm me.

"I'm ready to go. I'm tired and full." I say to him.

"Alright then. It's cool." He replies while starting the car and pulling out of the parking spot.

I sit back in silence, praying to myself. I haven't gotten these types of feelings since dealing with Marcus.

I know Marcus was doing me wrong, and the situations are different, but their intensity feels the same.

So, I'm trying to fight this off the only way I know how, and that's with God.

I think it's best I just go home, pray some more, and evaluate all these thoughts.

"Baby, I love you; there is no question about it. Everyone knows that I look to you as my wife; that girl and the past happened because I was reckless in not looking for a wife." He shares with me.

I sit back in silence some more. I'm emotional right now, and I don't want to say another thing out of emotion.

He grabs my hand while driving, and I hold on to him.

The drive home is longer due to traffic.

Omega continues to look at me; I know he's trying to read the expression on my face.

"You know you can say anything to me; whatever you want to ask, I'm here." He tells me assuredly.

My thoughts are consumed by what he used to do. I saw a glimpse of that life the night I met him. I think how soon before that was, he with her?

I'm wondering if it is possible for Kelsey to know of Cain and Rebecca.

I'm wondering about too many thoughts that are deep and dark like I would when I was dealing with Marcus and when I found out about an affair or something he did.

I know Omega is on another level, but the thoughts of what happened before me are there.

I know my thoughts aren't my own with the devil roaming around.

But this is also making me feel that maybe I'm still hurt by my past; that's why Omega's past bothers me so much.

Either way, I'm feeling saddened by this, and all I want to do is keep to myself.

"Will you ask me or talk to me if you have any questions?" Omega asks, breaking me out of my thoughts.

"Okay." I softly replied.

Omega played some music, but the rest of the drive home was silent between us.

Once we are back at my place, he opens the car door for me and then walks me to my apartment.

"How are you feeling? You were quiet the whole ride. You don't have to do that, and you have absolutely nothing to worry about." He tells me as he pulls me in for a hug.

I wrap my arms around his neck, hugging him back.

"Okay, I've just been thinking about a few things." I tell him while still in his embrace.

"Okay, then tell me about them." He says.

"I will once I get my thoughts together and get some rest." I explain it to him.

"Alright then, please let me know." He says.

He kisses me goodnight.

"I love you, babe." He says this before walking off.

"I love you too." I tell him.

I go inside my apartment and head to my room, where I sit down and begin to cry.

I lay back on the bed and prayed to God.

Heavenly Father, I need You. I thought those thoughts were gone. I was prepared to see a piece of Omega's past, and of course, it made me think of Rebecca Meyers. Help me clear my head and get some peaceful sleep. I want to think about what's pure, right, just, hopeful, and love. Please help us all think like that. I'm fighting to be the woman You want me to be, Lord. Please, Holy Spirit, guide me through this and all the rest You have for me. I love You. Amen.

I get off the bed, wash my face, and put my pajamas on before laying back in bed and going to sleep.

CHAPTER 24
For This Love

I woke to see two missed calls and a text message from Omega.

He always calls to say good night before bed, but I fell asleep from the tears after I said my prayer.

I get out of bed and get on my knees for prayer.

Good morning, Lord. Thank You for another day to fulfill Your will for Your glory and for breathing life into me to live another day here. I will progress in Your name, and I won't be defeated because I'm leaving it all in Your hands. I rebuke you, enemy, for getting in the way. Stay behind me, Satan; you have no life here. I love You, Lord. Amen.

I pick up my phone to call Omega.

"Hey baby, good morning. How are you?" He asks when he answers the phone.

"I'm doing good, just getting up. I said my prayer and was about to make some breakfast." I tell him.

"How are you?" I continue to ask him.

"I'm good, babe; I ate already, and I'm just getting a few things ready for the day." He says.

"Do you have any plans for later? I wanted to see you for a movie date." He asks.

"Yeah, sure, the movies sound fun." I respond to him.

"Do you want to pick the movie?" He asks me.

"Yeah, I will." I tell him.

"Okay, baby, check the movies and the times, and I'll get the tickets." He tells me.

"Okay, I will let you know." I tell him.

"Alright, I love you, babe. I'll talk to you later." He says.

"I love you too; bye." I say this before hanging up the phone.

I put the phone down and felt the waves of emotions come over me.

I held back, saying what was on my mind about the whole Kelsey encounter.

I went to sleep dwelling on it, but I slept well.

It was just as soon as I saw Omega's name on my phone that waves of feelings came back over me.

I go over to my study desk and grab my Bible. I need some encouragement from the one who bears all my troubles.

So, I read John 16:33. "In the world you will have tribulation. But take heart; I have overcome the world."

Isaiah 41:10: "So do not fear, for I am with you; do not be dismayed, for I am your God. I will strengthen you and help you; I will uphold you with my righteous right hand."

Philippians 4:6-7 Do not be anxious about anything, but in every situation, by prayer and petition, with thanksgiving, present your requests to God. And the peace of God, which transcends all understanding, will guard your hearts and your minds in Christ Jesus.

Romans 8:28 And we know that for those who love God all things work together for good, for those who are called according to His purpose.

I let the words saturate me; I really needed this uplifting.

I don't want to drag things out with Omega about his past and that I'm carrying my traumas from my past.

I'm still juggling to respond to my job offers and all that entails with possibly moving.

There are many church events that I need to start organizing with the rest of the group.

Omega has many critiques and social food events to attend, so I know we will both be busy the next couple of weeks.

And on top of it all, Rebecca Meyers's family wants to do another search in the community after they have put together some surveillance footage of her getting in her car.

All of this is a weight that God said I can put in His hands, and He'll bear it, smoothing it out to work for my good, Omega's good, Rebecca and her family, and for God to get all the glory.

I can't help but feel the stressors of it all.

And I don't want to put this on Ashley or my sister, my two girls I can talk to, because I know they will be in disbelief about Omega, and I don't want anyone to change their minds about him.

And they don't get the back story behind it; that's another reason why the information we are holding about Rebecca is heavy; Omega and I are carrying this alone.

So, hopefully, tonight's date night, we can talk all of this through.

I gather myself back and head to the kitchen to make breakfast.

I decide to make my famous omelet with a slice of toast and orange juice.

I play my worship music as I cook, dance and singing along to each song.

Giving God all the praise really does lift the spirit.

I eat and continue listening to music; I search for a movie on my phone.

I find a comedy at 7:15 PM; we love a great laugh, and the reviews are good.

I text Omega the details while I go to my room to take a shower.

After a long, hot shower, I check my phone and sit back to reply to a couple of text messages from my mom and Ashley

I put together some details for the upcoming Garden Ministries events and prepare for some other church organizations.

I go to my closet and pick out a pretty, white summer dress.

The time to meet with Omega is nearing, and while I am excited to see him, I still have nerves.

These are obvious signs that we need to talk, and this just might be our first big talk about our relationship.

We have had our ups and downs and little disagreements; we easily have gotten over them, but this issue has many hard factors entwined.

I finish getting ready, with my hair and makeup done.

Omega texted me to let me know he'll be arriving soon.

I pull myself together before I hear him knocking on the door.

I open the door to see his sweet, beautiful smile.

He has a beautiful bouquet of roses for me.

He's dressed in a nice pair of jean shorts and a light blue button-up T-shirt with a Gucci logo design all around.

He pulled me in for a tight hug and a kiss.

I'm always so moved by how he can hold me so tight in a hug and still hold the bouquet firmly in his hands.

"How are you beautiful?" He asks me as he releases me from his hold.

We walk into my kitchen so I can set the bouquet.

"I'm doing pretty well; I just wanted to get things done around the house today." I tell him.

"That's cool. Are you sure everything is alright?" He asks as he grabs my hand.

I want to be honest with him about what I'm thinking about, but I feel that he's not interested in speaking about that; he just wants to enjoy a night together.

So, I'll tell him what I'm feeling, when I can say it without being so emotional.

"I'm okay. I think I'm still trying to understand how I feel after all that action with Kelsey." I quickly said that to him.

No time wasted, I wanted to wait but part of my thoughts slipped out.

He takes a deep breath, and I can tell that was the reaction of someone not wanting to discuss something.

"I told you, baby; she doesn't matter here, and you have absolutely nothing to worry about." He says, then grabs both my hands.

"I know." I quietly say. I'm just not ready to go there with him.

"Okay, so let's go laugh, eat some good food, and connect more." He says.

This is going to be a battle.

But for now, this is a date night, so I grab my phone, purse, and keys as we walk to the door together.

The drive to the theater was quieter than usual, with slight tension in the air.

The music was playing softly as we liked; he was holding my hand like he does every drive, but I still felt the environment loading up with questions.

We have found a parking space, so there's no need for a valet.

We walk hand in hand to the theater.

And the place is beautiful, like an old, classic theater for performing arts.

I can't forget how Omega always seems to impress me, even when I least expect it because I never thought he would bring us to a place like this, let alone know that this would get me excited.

I know he knows me; he's my man, and he loves me.

"Ya, this is amazing; this is my first time here. I thought it would be cool to see a film in classical format." He says this to me.

"Yes, this is going to be so fun." I tell him with excitement.

I get relief as I feel myself coming back and the tension fading.

I just want to enjoy this with him.

"I know we are here much earlier than the show time, so I thought we could eat a little bit before the movie." He says, walking me to the pub restaurant.

I look to see an old Hollywood walk-a-fame type restaurant.

"This is so cute." I tell him exceedingly.

"Yeah, pretty cool." He says back, smiling and looking around.

We walk and get seated at the bar and agree to have one drink.

We enjoy whiskey drinks with no ice.

I felt it instantly and that relief.

"I feel better having this date night, so I can just let all that shit go." I say to him.

"What shit?" He asks me in a confused tone.

I can see an upset look on his face. The whiskey and bottled-up emotions are fighting me right now.

"You said you were cool, and you understand what's important, and that's you and me, not Kelsey's bullshit." He continues to say.

I think now of how I should reply.

"It did bother me to have an ex interact with you so deeply. I feel like if it really was what you say it was, a girl you were just seeing, not a serious relationship, then she wouldn't have acted that way." I finally say.

"She's mad that she's not you and she went on and continued doing all the shit that didn't put her up to your level." He quickly responds.

And his response didn't make me feel the way I assumed he was trying to make me feel.

"Omega, that sounded like you were hoping she would be." I say to him.

"Don't even try to twist that up. You know I meant just that, and I wouldn't marry someone who's spiraling with drugs and alcohol." He says this to me.

"So, if she wasn't doing that, would it have worked out?" I ask him.

"Of course not; otherwise, it would have happened that way. We talk about God leading you to the right shit and if she was right, it would have worked out, things happen for a reason even the fucked up things." He says back at me.

"None of that was feeling right, and I can't help but feel this way." I say to him.

"Why are you twisting this up?" He asks me sharply.

"Because I don't deal with ex's and females approaching me and whatever drama, I had much of that, and it never gets anywhere." I tell him.

"You can think whatever, but you're in your head with all of this." He says this to me.

"Every time we go out, Omega, some woman is trying to get closer to you. I ignore them because they don't know you. But Kelsey knew you, and she knew a dark part of you, which was a big part of you." I say to him.

This conversation officially made us late for the movie.

"None of that matters, and I don't care because that has nothing to do with me now." He replies.

"Was she there around the time your brother died? Could she have possibly known about Rebecca and Cain too? And with all the sex you too probably had, I'm sure she has some weird soul-tie connection to you." I say, coming out with it all.

He looks at me, giving me a look that he's never given me before.

With a look of disappointment, I knew he wasn't feeling what I had to say.

"Look, I love you, but you're way off. Something is stressing you with all of these thoughts, and it's not cool." He says this to me.

I now get upset.

He can't blame me or get bothered by what I have to say.

Omega blowing off my feelings is really hurting me now. We are supposed to share feelings without judgment.

"Yeah, because all this shit is serious. And it's not like you confirmed that she probably doesn't know what you know about

Rebecca. I feel that the case is jumping out everywhere, and now a ghost of your past comes up out of nowhere, basically demanding you to come back like it's so easy or she has you for something." I say to him.

Omega just sits back and stares into space; I can tell he's thinking something.

"I know what all of this could be, and I told you because it was heavy on me; I'm the only person that saw them last, and that was tough on me, and I trusted your support. None of this was for you to start taking off at the smallest inconvenience and insulting my intelligence as if I'm not thinking about this case from every angle." He says this to me.

"Well, if you had shit under control, she wouldn't have popped up," I say, right back at him.

"Wow, there's things I shouldn't have told you because clearly you can't handle them in a mature way. This is surprising coming from a woman who hears from God." He says this to me with anger.

"Okay, now you are insulting me, and you really think it would be cool to be with me and keep that in the dark." I say.

"I don't know, but what I do know is that you're carrying feelings that reflect some past issue you have because you're not hearing my answers, just wanting to go off on your feelings. You're probably afraid of it happening again and what we did during that time, but more than anything, this shows me that you still really don't know me. I'm not going back into any of that." He says this while barely looking at me.

We both sit back in silence.

I don't know what to really say now, mainly because he was speaking the truth.

At this point, I'm lost for time and the movie is probably almost over.

"You told me I could be honest with my feelings, but I feel judged. I don't like this." I say to him.

The tension from earlier is back ten times worse, and I can also feel us holding back some mean things we want to say to each other.

"Yeah, I'm not feeling this shit either. I let go of all that because I wanted to move on and be happy, hoping to find someone like you, and I'm blessed to have you in all of this. Now you're telling me that you don't like something I'm done with, even when that means we have each other to get through things." He says this while standing up.

"This is bigger than you and me, Omega. Kelsey coming back around was to remind us that we still have demons within us and around us; they need to be rebuked. We can't live on our own cloud anymore." I say to him.

"We have control over what we choose to consume us." He quickly says.

"No God has all control; we've just been pretending like we do." I tell him.

"Whatever, I'm done with this shit, and I'm ready to go." He says.

"Yeah, I feel that too. If you can, please just take me home." I say as I walk past him, heading towards the car.

We missed the movie, didn't have any dinner, and were full of anger.

We've never been like this before; I never seen him look so mad.

He follows behind me as we walk to the car.

I'm trying not to cry.

I get into the car, and so does he, starting the engine and heading home to drop me off.

No music or a word said the whole ride back.

As soon as we pull up to my apartment complex and he parks, I quickly get out and walk to my door.

I didn't have anything more to say to him tonight.

I hear him get out of the car.

"You know I don't want you to walk alone to your door." He shouts.

"I'm good, I can make it." I say, and I don't even look back.

At this point, I'm full of tears.

I get inside my apartment, throw my things down, and go to lie in bed.

The tears have made me drowsy, and I fall asleep crying out for Omega and the Lord.

I woke up still wearing my dress and makeup from last night.

I grab my phone and see missed calls and texts from Omega.

He said he wanted to talk some more and that he would wait out front for me.

He even said he knocked on the door.

It was heavy on my soul, and I slept through it all.

Although I'm upset, I feel terrible that he was out there knocking.

But I needed that rest.

I go into my bathroom and take a shower.

The shower was long and warm, washing all that arguing off from last night.

I go into my closet to grab some comfy lounge clothes.

I'm still feeling sad about all that happened between Omega and me.

We have never argued before, and he's never been upset with me or I, him.

I sit back on my couch, holding my pillow as tears start coming down my cheeks.

I think back on what we said to each other last night.

We said things we shouldn't have, but it was in the heat of the moment.

But what saddened me most was how defensive he was becoming over me asking about the possibility of Kelsey knowing that he has information on Rebecca's last whereabouts.

I thought I could express myself, no matter what the situation may be, with Omega.

And I know people don't like talking about their past relationships, but Kelsey seems a bit more involved than he admits.

I lay back, contemplating all of this. I know my feelings are valid. And I will take responsibility for bringing my past traumas upon Omega.

It is clear that there is more growing for both of us to do.

And I know I need space to clear all this up, and I'm sure he needs it more.

I don't have much of an appetite and have decided to just lie back and watch TV.

As the day went on, I talked to my grandma. Ashley, April, and I had to hold back all that happened with Omega and me because no one knew about the information he had.

Omega and I said we would keep it between us and God.

Now, I feel like I don't have anyone to talk to because I must keep this quiet.

My hunger kicks in, and I warm up some leftover food.

I got ready and went to bed.

As I began to get under the covers, I started to cry as I whispered, 'Jesus.'

The next couple of days were slow and tearful.

Omega hasn't reached out.

I tried to keep myself busy by going over more plans for Garden Ministries.

I also tried to give myself a deadline for sending a follow-up regarding the job offers.

I wanted to talk to Omega about the offers because they all involved me moving around more than usual.

It was hard to decide, not knowing what that would mean for our relationship.

But now it's coming up that my lease is changing, and the remaining trust fund for my living costs is almost out, and I don't want to touch the money I have for savings.

I'm trying not to be too hard on myself, but I slacked off. I should have had all this planned out.

I also don't have anyone to share this with since it is all attached to what Omega, and I are holding.

After about a week of mourning my relationship and battling confusion and doubt, I start to get ready for the night after deciding to go out for a drink.

I just want to be alone, so I don't even ask Ashley to join.

I chose to go to Spence's, the place that means a lot to me, as that's where Omega and I first met.

That lounge, that night changed my life, but it was mostly him.

I'm not having more than one drink, so I'll be fine to drive.

I'm dressed in a cute pair of Levi jeans and my white ruffled top.

I'm super casual and comfortable enough to enjoy getting out of the house.

I played my R&B gospel the whole drive there and found a good parking spot near the entrance.

I arrive to a nice crowd of people hanging out.

I walk straight to the top and see that everything looks the same.

I went over to the bar, found a seat, and soaked up the environment.

I ordered a martini, something I normally never drink but wanted to try tonight.

I sit back and hang out with my drink in my hand, enjoying the night.

People are dancing, and couples are holding each other close.

I have gotten some drink offers, and some have come to ask me to dance.

I firmly turn them down.

I look over to see a man intensely looking at me.

I'm not here for that; I want Omega, and I'm still very much in love.

We just needed our space, and I needed to get out of the house.

I look over and see the guy looking more and more.

He was a white man, maybe in his late 20s or early 30s, wearing jeans and a black T-shirt.

I could tell he was a bit toasty from his drinks.

As he continues to stare, I look back and all around me to see if it's me he's really looking at.

I then look back, and he signals that I'm the one he's looking at and winks at me.

I take the rest of my drink back and grab my purse to leave.

As soon as I stood up, I felt every ounce of the martini.

I turn back to the bartender and ask for a glass of water.

When he hands it to me, and I start to drink, I feel a pull on my arm, and it's the man who was staring at me.

I pull from his release and give him an uncomfortable look.

"Why are you touching me?" I ask him.

"I've been wanting you all night." He says it while mumbling other words.

"No, thank you; I'm good and leaving," I tell him that as I finish my water, I can go now.

"I'll take you home, and you can show me how the pretty little body looks without clothes on." He says.

"You lost your mind; that's not going to happen. You need a ride home yourself with your drunken ass." I shout at him.

"Well, take me home so I can punish that mouth for cussing at me." He says this while getting closer.

"Get out of your crazy mind and go to God." I say, pushing through him to walk.

As I near the stairs to the exit, I feel my arm being grabbed again.

And I look to see it's him, looking furious.

"Don't grab me like that," I say, pulling away.

"I don't appreciate you disrespecting me and then trying to talk about God. What do you think you're some righteous person? Well, I'll tell you what you look like: a woman sitting at the bar waiting for a man to approach her and go home to fuck." He shouts.

"You're out of your mind, and you don't even know me." I tell.

The song changed; it was louder, and I couldn't make out what he was saying now.

"Get behind me, Satan." I shouted aloud to him.

"Yeah, I will, and I'll fuck that attitude right out of you." He says it with so much anger.

And I felt that I was looking Satan in the eyes.

Why am I the only one seeing this?

I turn to quickly walk away; I try to reach into my purse to grab my phone.

He again grabbed my arm really hard; this time, I fell and hit the ground.

Fear was running through my body, and I put my hands up for protection when I looked up to see him standing over me.

I closed my eyes and then opened them when I heard a loud, crashing sound.

I see Omega jumping down onto the man, hitting him over and over.

The crowd was starting to stir around and trample over me. I felt myself getting kicked around and drinks falling over me, and I instantly started to scream, but the chaos was so loud no one heard me.

I couldn't see Omega anymore at this point.

I'm trying my hardest to get up and gather myself, but I keep getting pushed around.

It seems like everyone is fighting now.

All I want is Omega at this point.

I feel myself getting weak; I think it's a combination of the drink and all the fear this situation has caused.

The music stops, and the crowd starts to clear when security rushes in.

I'm still on the floor, and someone reaches down to help me up and then tells me that I'm bleeding from my head.

I touch my head and see the blood.

I think I did knock out for a minute.

Now that the police are here, I see them rush in, taming the crowd.

I still don't see Omega.

I try to make my way over to a cop for help when I see paramedics rush in, too.

Someone must be hurt; where is Omega?

I finally get a glimpse of Omega, and he's stumbling to get up as the paramedics check him out.

I rush over to him.

"Baby, are you okay?" I ask him.

He's holding his side, and by the look on his face, I could tell he was in pain.

"He stabbed me." Omega moans out.

I start crying.

"You're bleeding too." He says this to me.

I start to feel myself having a panic attack.

The paramedic grabs me and then yells for assistance.

Omega tries to grab me, but I just close my eyes.

My eyes are shut, it's dark, it's silent.

I wake up with Ashley standing over me, talking to a nurse.

I'm in the hospital, lying in bed, but I don't have a gown on.

I'm still wearing the clothes I wore.

Once they noticed I was awake.

Ashley quickly pulls me in for a hug.

"Are you okay?" You scared us so bad? What is going on Sunday?" Ashley continues to ask.

"You were hit with a glass bottle, knocked out and had a panic attack at Spence's." She continues to say.

"I'm okay, I tell her, where is Omega?" I ask her.

"We needed to have your vitals checked and make sure you aren't suffering from a concussion." The nurse speaks in to say.

"Okay, where is Omega?" I ask again, trying to stand up.

"Ma'am, before I release anything to you, I must make sure you are okay. Where are you?" The nurse asks.

"In the hospital." I quickly responded.

"What's today's date?" The nurse asks again.

"It's Thursday, August 20th, 2023." I respond again.

"What's your mother's name?" She asks me.

"Deborah." I remark.

"When is your birthday?" She asks.

"January 2nd, 1997," I tell her.

"Okay, thank you." She says.

"Where is Omega?" I quickly asked her again.

"He's down in hall room 203. He's healing up from his procedure…" The nurse says.

I start to walk off after hearing the room number; that's all I need—to be with him. I don't care about the rest.

Ashley is following behind me.

"What is going on Sunday? How is it that you both end up in the hospital? What kind of fight happened at Spence's?" Ashley goes on to ask many questions.

It's not that I'm trying to ignore her; it's just that there's a lot to explain, and I really need to get to Omega first.

"I will tell you, Ashley, I promise. I just have to check on Omega right now. And I'm very thankful that you are here." I tell her as I walk, getting closer to Omega's room.

I walk into the room to see Omega lying up in the bed; his shirt is off, and from the looks of it, he has a bandage from the stab womb.

Nick is talking with him, and they both look over at Ashely and me as we walk in.

I run up to hug.

"Hi baby, Are you alright? I'm so sorry you're here like this." I told him, embracing him as I began to cry.

"I'm good I'm happy to see you, baby; I've been waiting for you." He tells me.

"Are you okay?" I ask him again.

"I had to get stitches where that asshole stabbed me. Didn't hit anything major, thank God." He says.

"Yes, thank You, Lord. I'm so glad you're okay." I tell him while still holding him in a hug.

"I was trying to get out of here to see you, but the nurses threatened to tie me down if I didn't sit still; it got rowdy in here. I don't think they like me in this hospital and are ready for me to leave." He tells me, and we both start to giggle.

"Baby, I love you, and I'm so sorry about all of this. I know we have to talk." I tell him.

"Yeah, we need to talk. Come home with me when we get released." He says.

"I love you, Sunday." He continues to say.

Ashley and Nick gave us our space for the next couple of hours.

Omega and I continued to comfort each other until the nurse brought out release forms.

Nick had ordered a ride share for us to use one of his cars so Omega and I could get to his house and get our cars from Spence's later.

We all hugged and said goodbye.

Omega held my hand as I drove us to his house.

CHAPTER 25
From the Beginning to the End

We have been at Omega's house for the past three days, resting and healing.

The stabbing he suffered was deep, but we've been thanking God over and over for sparing him any severe damage.

I've been cooking and helping him clean up.

Ashley and Nick called to check in a couple of times; they can tell we've been short on explanations and are still giving us our space.

We haven't told our families much of anything yet because they will have many questions that Omega and I aren't ready to answer.

We still owe each other that deep conversation before explaining it to anyone else.

I sleep in Omega's bed, and he sleeps in the extra bedroom.

Throughout the night, we come to check on each other.

Avoiding the talk has made it easier for our bodies to heal, but we know we must soon begin the soul-healing process of finally discussing what has been going on with us.

Our secrets have led us to both shed blood, remain distant, and lack justice.

While I was making lunch for us, I made the decision to tell him I was ready to talk.

I make the table and place our sandwiches and chips down for us.

I made sweet tea, which we both love so much.

"Thank you, baby; this looks good." Omega says this when he comes into the kitchen.

He gives me a gentle kiss on the lips.

I wish we could stay in this world forever, with no problems, where we just stay in the house, eat, and comfort one another.

But that's not freedom; that's not walking out as a servant of God.

We enjoy the food and small conversation.

We clean the kitchen together, and I pull Omega in for a hug and kiss.

I kiss him passionately, with warmth and sensation.

I really do love this man, and sharing our little intimacy is important.

Our healing and juggling of thoughts have prevented us from making that connection we need so bad.

"Wow, baby, I like that." He says this while kissing me.

I know that eventually, we will have to stop and put down the fleshy feelings that are beginning to arise.

"I do too." I say to him.

"You know we gotta stop and calm down, though." He says this to me.

"Yes, I know." I say back to him.

He loses his embrace and grabs my hand as we walk over to the couch. We sit close and in silence.

"I know it's time for us to talk about all of this." He says, breaking the silence.

"Yes, I know." I say it again in agreement.

"I'm going to start." He says.

"Okay," I respond.

Everything we have is determined by this conversation.

"I know the Rebecca Meyers case has been a hold on us since I told you what I knew. But there is more to it; I need to tell you." He softly says.

I start to feel the tears come up, and my throat tightens.

I continue to sit back and listen.

"Cain started seeing her to help him push drugs. He was telling me about this girl he met: she was young, she needed extra money, she was trying to get away from home, and all that. I had never seen her then. I know they were doing a lot of drugs, and he would tell me she was into everything. Multiple times, he asked me to help them move product to the food vendors I was working with so they could do back-door deals. Cain was certain those guys had a fix and had the money to buy whatever they wanted. I was hesitant because I knew how hard they were indulging, and although I was dealing myself with the alcohol, I knew the shit was wrong but never said anything. The day before she went missing, I finally saw her, and even though she had a nice bag and shoes, you could tell she was deep in whatever she and Cain were doing and unhappy. I met up with Cain to help him out with his car, and she was there and didn't say anything to me. She just sat around, looking faded." He tells me.

My mind is running with thoughts.

I see him straighten up; I can tell he's getting choked up.

"Cain came to me panicking, like a day or two after the reports went out of her missing, saying that Rebecca fucked up badly. He said she left a party drunk and upset because her and her mom were fighting. She was trying to find Cain, but he said he was busy doing things, so she drove off. She came to him the next morning crying hysterically because she hit someone. And this was the morning after my brother was hit and killed, but I could tell Cain was twisted up on some drug, and so I didn't want to put in his head that it was Rebecca who hit Max. I always knew it, though." He goes on to say.

We're both having tears come down our faces.

It makes sense how Rebecca's mom said she was panicking when she came to her and the dent in the front of the car.

I stayed in silence. I put my hand on his back to bring him comfort.

"It was confirmed that a black woman in a red car hit Max after the detective spoke with my parents when they were last here. They haven't really been following the Rebecca case, so they don't know about her missing. The same car she hit Max in was the same car that Cain and I were working on a couple of days before all the shit happened. I asked Cain where Rebecca was after she hit someone, and he said she was hiding out at one of his operation houses. I talked with him about getting clean and clearing his name, and he got defensive, I guess feeling like I was going to tell on him. He left, then came back a couple of days later after finding out that it was Max who Rebecca hit and killed. He felt bad, came back crying and stressing, and said that he handled her. He took her to some sunset bridge and made her apologize, but he said she was acting scary and wanted help, and they began to fight, so he pushed her over. Then, drove the car back and left some evidence of a shoe to throw off any searches. I got so mad, and we began to fight, but he pulled his gun out of his bag and faced it at me. He then ran out, and I haven't seen him since." He continues to say.

I sat shocked, tears rolling down my face. I'm motionless and speechless.

Omega knew way more than he originally told me.

This is terrible and explains the heaviness accumulated since meeting him and being involved with Rebecca's case.

He knows enough to lead investigators to possibly find her body, bringing justice and peace to her family and his.

He has also been carrying the grief of Max while really knowing that it was Rebecca who killed him.

This whole time, he's been holding back.

Although this hurts, and I feel lied to, too, I understand even more the darkness and demons that were following him.

But I also saw how he was trying to get closer to God through all of this.

"I'm sorry I didn't tell you about any of this Sunday. I didn't want to hurt you anymore. I'm ashamed, I'm fucked up, and you helped me feel pieced together, leading me back to God and to vision. I just wanted all of this to go away. I didn't want anyone else to get hurt." Omega says while crying.

We both sit there crying.

I want to say something but don't know what to say.

So, I just grab his hand and hold it; he grabs on and holds tight.

I feel the Holy Spirit come over me with some words to say.

"I'm so sorry about Max and you having to hold back on his killer." I finally say it to him.

He nods his head, still crying.

"God is building you, even when things are breaking you." I tell him.

We come closer to each other for a hug.

He's never cried to me like this before.

I feel his heaviness. I hold him even tighter so he knows I'm here for him.

"It's okay, Omega; God is going to work everything out." I tell him.

"Just the way it's supposed to be." I continue.

He pulls back, wiping away his tears; his face is red and sad.

"I'm so sorry about all of this." I say to him.

"No, I'm sorry for holding back all of this. I know you would've been supportive if I told you sooner. I've just been scared honestly because I know the right thing to do is now tell the authorities what I know. All this time has been passing, and the case is getting colder, and they need the information. I just know I'm going to be a suspect and will get questioned." He says.

I don't know what to say because I don't want to lose him, but he needs to do the right thing, the godly thing.

"I will be here for you." I tell him with certainty.

He nods his head.

I know it's hard for him to believe that.

"I want to share something with you." I began to tell him.

"It has been eating at me—all the information we were keeping about Rebecca, especially because I was so involved with the case. I was seeking something to do while I was waiting for the teacher's administration to call about a job. I couldn't explain why I got so connected to this case, but I always felt it was because there was more to the story and all I had to do was figure out what that more was. When you explained to me what you knew and I decided to keep my word and not say anything with you about her, it made sense to me. This girl hurt a huge part of my future, which was you. I can't even make big decisions right now because it all matters having you in my life, and these decisions will affect us. I have gotten job offers, but they are not local and would take me away from you, and I couldn't make my mind up, so it was driving me crazy. It seems like things were clear not too long ago, but now I want different things, and I'm at the point where those different things have to involve you, or I don't want them. And I mostly feel like if I'm not with you, bad things will happen, like it did the other night at Spencer's." I tell him.

I began to cry, and he brought me in and held me.

"I feel that we just made a huge step in sharing this with each other, and now we must do what's right. And we know God does not give us overcoming life, He gives us life as we overcome. We exhibited the ultimate sacrifice to each other when we got hurt at Spence's, so now we really need to give this relationship to God and stop trying to produce in our own strength. I'm going to the police station today and tell them what I know. And you are going to pick the very best job offer. And then we are going to have to trust that God will bring us back together if it is His will. Nothing will be able to separate us if His will is in this. I know you said you want different things now, but I know you have a deep passion to help kids and lead the next generation to know God. That's what's right, and you helped me see the light, so I can only imagine what you can do for those kids. And I must do what's right. I was freed from drug and alcohol spiraling. He'll get me through this. This is how we become stronger individuals for each other." Omega says to me.

I'm trying to hold my sobs in; it's grief that I'm experiencing.

"Okay," is all I'm able to say.

"It kills me to see you cry." He says.

He wraps his arms around me and begins to give me forehead kisses.

We sit like this for 20 minutes.

"Let's go, baby. I'm going to take you home and head to the police station." Omega says as he lets me go and stands up to grab my hand.

I take hold of his hand and follow him to the room to grab my things.

I have no words.

This is hard, but he's right.

We freshen up in the bathroom, and he grabs his phone, keys, and wallet, and then we head out the door to his truck.

He opens the passenger side door for me and makes sure I'm seated.

I started to remember the first time I came here to give him his beanie back.

All our memories are beautiful.

He gets in on the driver's side, gives me a small smile, and begins to back out of the driveway.

"Oh, look, it's my Tokyo beanie I was wearing the first night we met." He says this while reaching out and grabbing.

"I was just thinking of that beanie." I tell him.

"Really, then it is special; I'm going to wear it to the station." He says, and this time, he gives me an even bigger smile.

He holds my hand during the car ride; the radio is on, but I'm not listening to what's playing.

Once we arrive at my home, he walks me up to my door.

"Let's say a prayer." I tell him.

"Okay." He says it in agreement.

"Dear Heavenly Father. We thank You for never leaving us and always guiding us. We have come to a point where the only thing we can do is leave things in Your hands. And we know this is what You have wanted all this time. We thank You for the overwhelming grace and love You freely give us. We seek Your peace and wisdom more than anything. With the true desire of being consumed by Your presence. Please protect us on the next steps and mostly let Your will be done. We love You. Amen."

"Amen." Omega says in agreement.

He pulls me in for a tight hug and kisses me passionately.

"I love you, Sunday; I always will." He says this to me.

"I love you too." I say back to him.

He lets me go and heads down the hallway towards the exit.

I open my door, head to my couch, and lay down and cry.

Crying myself to sleep.

I woke up, and it was almost 8 p.m.

I slept for almost 6 hours.

I saw my notifications, but I didn't hear my phone at all.

I check to see if any of them are from Omega.

I just saw texts from April and Ashley.

I know everyone wants to know what's going on with us, but all I care about is getting things right with Omega.

I go to my room to take a shower.

While I was there, I started to decide which job I should take. I'm really leaning toward being a youth counselor.

Once I'm out the shower, I put some comfortable pajamas on and tie up my hair. I then hear a knock on my door.

And it sounds like Omega's knock.

He would have called though.

I walk to the door and check the peephole, and I see it is him, still wearing his beanie.

I open the door, and he immediately grabs me and picks me up, spinning me around.

"What's going on?" I ask him when he finally settles me down.

"They questioned me, had me in interrogation for hours, stood over me, tried to tear me down, but couldn't find anything to keep me for." He says it with excitement.

"I know they're going to be contacting Rebecca's family, and they'll know the truth soon." He continues to say.

"Oh, thank God, baby, I'm so glad it's working out." I tell him, then grab his face for a kiss.

"I need you to come with me somewhere right now." He quickly says.

"What, wait, baby, I have to change; I just put my pajamas on." I tell him as I start walking back to my room.

"No, baby, I love the pajamas; I love how comfortable you look; please just come with me." He says.

"Okay then." I'm kind of confused, but I love his passion.

I know he's feeling safe and proud, and I want to keep that energy up with him.

I'll follow his lead with this.

I put my slides on, grabbed my things, and went with him.

"What's going on, baby?" I ask him as we get into the car.

"You'll see." He says.

He holds my hand as we drive while some of our songs play in the background.

The drive kept me full of anticipation as we got closer to the coast, where we were surrounded by a starry sky, ocean sounds, and a night breeze.

He opens the door to get out and then walks over to help me out of the car.

He then goes to his trunk, where I see a picnic in preparation.

"Wow, baby, look at this." I say this to him in amusement.

He has candles, champagne, flowers, and ramen.

He finishes setting it all up, and we have a romantic picnic under the stars.

We laughed the whole time; this date felt better than any date before.

"Come on, let's get closer to the water." He says, grabbing my hand and kissing it.

We are both looking out into the night water and the big, bright, starry sky; it's so peaceful.

"There's nowhere in life I can go without you, and Sunday life is with you." He looks at me and says.

Then he gets down on one knee, pulls out a beautiful red velvet box, and opens it.

"Will you marry me?" He asks me.

I start to cry, saying yes over and over again.

He puts the ring on my finger and kisses me.

We are both crying, full of emotions, but mostly love.

I looked at my beautiful ring.

It's a stunning diamond in a round shape, almost looking to be in the shape of a rose.

He holds me with a big hug, and we walk back to his truck.

I have the biggest smile on my face.

We decide to camp out, lying in the bed of his truck, drinking champagne, and talking about life for the rest of the night.

The peace in the middle of our storm.

CHAPTER 26
It is Done

We woke up early from the cool morning ocean breeze.

Omega was holding me warmly under the blanket.

I look at my hand, admiring my ring and the uniqueness it holds.

"I know there is a story behind the ring. I haven't seen all the rings in the world, but I'm most confident it's the prettiest one." I tell him.

"I designed it with my mom's jeweler and picked the diamond about 2 months after meeting you. I told my mom I was going to marry you." He says.

I turn to look at him.

"Wow, thank you, husband." I give him a tight hug.

It felt so affirming to say that.

We loaded up our things and headed back home.

I felt so full, like a new woman, an engaged woman.

Throughout the drive, Omega would hold my hand, and I would look at and admire my ring. Then I would look to admire him, so thankful for God creating him.

Once we make it to his home, we unload the truck and take a shower. I began making lunch for us.

And throughout the day, we called my family, who knew because Omega had asked my father for my hand.

They were screaming and shouting for our joy.

We called Omega's family; they were thrilled, and we talked to Ashley and Nick.

Ashley and Nick have been very supportive friends, not pushing for information as they know we are dealing with things and not sharing as much as we normally would.

We know we can't tell them about the case now, so we focused the conversation on the engagement and that's why Omega has been so distant.

They're so happy for us, and I can tell they felt so peaceful knowing we were okay after the altercation that led us to the hospital the other night at Spence's.

When I was with Marcus, I spilled everything about our relationship with Ashley.

Now, with my growth, I see how unnecessary and disrespectful that is. Privacy is key.

Whether it was an unhealthy relationship in the past or something even better now, sharing everything doesn't get you anywhere if no change is being made.

Omega and I said we would wait to tell the pastor about the engagement on Sunday.

We ate lunch and cleaned the kitchen together.

We then lay on the couch, sharing intimate kisses, still refraining from sex until our wedding night.

Omega found movies to watch as we fell asleep.

For the next couple of days, Omega and I stayed in the house lounging.

I told him about my job offers, specifically the youth counselor offer, that I was interested in taking.

He confirmed that he would be right there for me, and we would figure out how to make it all happen.

Our schedules would cause us to be apart more now that I wouldn't be working in town, and his job takes him all around the city.

Omega and I planned for our first date tonight as his fiancé's.

We made reservations at a steakhouse.

I got dressed in his guest bedroom, and he went into his room.

I bought a red dress that fits like a glove. It has gold outline trimmings and is strapless with a low back.

I have gold shoes and earrings to match.

As I was getting ready, Omega came knocking on the guest bedroom door, holding his phone.

"Hey, babe, my security camera is showing 2 police cars parked out with about 4 cops." He says it with worry on his face.

'What!" I am startled.

The doorbell rang, and someone was knocking.

"Damn, they came for me." He says, stressing.

"What's going on, baby?" I ask while I start to cry.

"I don't know." He says this as he leaves the room and runs down the stairs.

I quickly follow behind him.

Once he reaches the door, Omega opens it and looks directly at the cops.

"What's going on?" He asks them.

"You're under arrest for the conspiracy to kill Rebecca Meyers." The first cop says as he pushes through the door, grabbing Omega and turning him to handcuff.

The other cops follow, giving the first cop support.

I start to shout at the cops.

"What's going on? He never conspired against Rebecca." I tell the cops.

Omega starts to hustle around and pull from the cops, and I see them begin to use more force to hold him down.

"Now he's fighting back." One officer shouts as he throws Omega down to the floor.

I start to scream more.

I run up to try to get close to Omega, and one of the other officers grabs me and bends me down over the couch.

I start to scream in pain.

I hear Omega yelling at the cops to let me go.

The officer finally let me off once the other three cops got Omega up from the floor and out the door.

The cop holding me down lets me go and heads out after them, not saying anything to me.

He leaves the door open, so I hear them start the vehicles and take off.

I fall to the ground, crying.

I don't know what to do or who to call because no one knows that Omega is involved in this.

"Please, Lord, give me Your strength and wisdom; what do I do?" I ask aloud as tears roll down my face.

I felt the Holy Spirit guide me, so I got up and went to change my dress.

I'm Omega's fiancé, and I should have some rights to information on him.

I get the keys to the car and head to the police station.

I talk and pray to God the whole way there.

Once I arrive, I get out of the car and run into the police station.

I found the reference and information desk immediately.

"Hello, I'm looking for information on my fiancé Omega Williams; he was just arrested at our home." I quickly said this to the lady.

She looked unfazed by my urgency.

"Okay, what's his name again?" She asks sternly.

"Omega Williams. You may have just seen him; he has long, curly brown hair. They should have come in right before I got here." I say as I take a look down the hallways.

"No, not yet; I don't have anything to share." She says.

"How? He was just arrested. I don't think I got here before them." I say it in a confused manner.

"Well, you can take a seat and wait it out, or he might have gone to another station." She implies.

"The only other station would be almost 45 minutes from here." I tell her.

"Well, like I said, you can have a seat; maybe they are not in yet." She quickly says.

"Okay." I jump back at her aggressiveness and sit down.

It feels like I've been sitting for hours.

I checked the time on my phone, and it's been two whole hours, but there is still no Omega.

The clerk officer at the desk hasn't said anything to me since I walked in and asked her about Omega.

My suspicions are rising, my soul feels worried, and I continue to pray, searching for God in this.

I'm tired, hungry, and uncomfortable after sitting here for almost 5 hours.

No one has acknowledged me; I've seen other people come in from being arrested, and I hear the police radio going off about other cases.

I stand up and walk over to the information and receptionist counter.

"Is there still no information you can share with me? I've been here for hours." I tell the same lady who was rude to me when I first walked in.

I feel so defeated, but Omega is my fiancé now, and I must fight for him.

"Nope." She quickly says this without looking at me.

I lean down on the counter, pressing into her more.

It's time for her to know me.

"I need your name and the contact information of your supervisor." I tell her sternly.

"Why?" She asks with a bass tone.

"I'm going to continue to follow up on where my husband is, and since you can't give me anything useful, I will speak with your supervisor." I tell her.

"He's busy, and if there is anything to share, we'll call you." She says back.

"I will riot this place up." I snap back at her.

"Take the card." She says as she tosses the card on the counter in front of me.

"Thank you." I remark as I turn to walk out.

Thank you for not letting it get any more difficult, Father.

I drove back to Omega's home, hoping he had returned.

It's dark out; there are no lights on, so no Omega.

I go to lie down on the couch, trying not to cry because I'm getting sick of crying. I'm waiting to hear a word from God on what to do about this; I'm waiting for Him to intercede.

I can't call anyone now; there is no trace of where he has gone, and the only help I thought I could get from the police station was hostile.

I start falling into a deep sleep. So tired from all these tears.

The sudden knocking on the door startled me.

The early morning cool breeze was coming through the house. I passed out on the couch and didn't close the windows.

It felt like it was about 6 a.m.

Was I dreaming, or was that really a knock at the door?

I look out the peephole and don't see anything.

It must have been a dream. I check my phone to see notifications, but nothing about Omega, so it doesn't interest me.

It's almost been a whole day since the police came for Omega.

I know I'm going to have to call his family, or they will be calling soon.

His phone is dead, so I connect it to the charger.

A thought crosses my mind: once Omega's phone comes back on, I can check the cameras to see for a badge name on one of the officers.

I got another notification on my phone alerting me that my phone needed a charge soon.

I remembered that my other charger was still in Omega's truck.

I get up and walk to the door. I open it, but when I take a step down, I hear the noise of a stem breaking.

I looked to see a single white rose, and I had stepped on it, breaking apart the stem.

The single white rose has a note tied to it and wrapped around it in a white ribbon.

Could this be Omega?

He always has roses for me; it's never been a single rose, always a bouquet.

And white roses were very rare for him to bring; the few times he brought them were random, or at least I thought.

Why would he come and leave a rose at the front door and not say anything to me?

He must know I'm worried, sick, and eating my tears.

Plus, I'm holding all this information with no direction to go.

I quickly pick it up and walk back into the house.

I untie the note from the white ribbon, releasing it from the rose.

I open the curled note to see the words in writing.

I have to go get justice for all the wrongs I tried to right; that's the only way God can fight this battle for me. I love you. Trust the journey that is right in God's eyes.

I feel like my ears are clogged, my eyes go blurry, and I feel a pain coming from the root of my gut that I have never felt before.

This was Omega, and he did come here, and he didn't come in to see me or get his phone, wallet, or anything.

This was Omega, and so I know that there is more to this than him just leaving me.

I'm his fiancé; I have all his information; I'm in his home; there is nothing I don't have access to.

Which means this was possibly deliberated.

I trust that he won't leave me like this; I must help him.

Something is going on, and it looks like we're about to face our giant.

His phone vibrates, signaling that it is on, so now I can check the cameras to get the name badge of the police that were there and to see him on the camera, leaving the rose and the note.

I know the code for his phone; he has openly shared it with me.

I went to his security camera app and rewind a few hours ago when I heard the knock on the door this morning; obviously, it wasn't a dream.

It's a man I don't recognize, but mostly because he has a hoody on, and his face is low.

I don't know if Omega would be trying to cover his face purposefully.

And he quickly sets the rose down, knocks on the door, and walks away.

I rewind to the footage from yesterday when the police officers came to the door.

But almost 30 minutes before all the officers presumed the front door, the same figure with a hoody on walks to the front door, and it's Omega. He seems to be checking for something around the door.

I can't tell because it's out of camera view from there.

I dropped his phone and ran to the door. I opened the door to look around like Omega seemed to be doing in the camera footage.

And I see a small black book stored underneath some plant vines above the entrance of the door.

I walk back into the house with it in my hand.

I scan through quickly and briefly read what seems to be a confessional, and at the back are lawyers' names, account numbers, and home addresses located in different parts of the country and some in other countries.

Omega put this there right before the police came. So, he must have known something was about to happen and left it there for me.

This is a war, and Omega is leaving me the tools to help him fight, but first, I need to find him.

But above all else, I must pray.

~Ending Part One~

Part two:

God's Purpose for Sunday

Will be released soon.

Thank you for reading

Sincerely,

Tiese

www.ingramcontent.com/pod-product-compliance
Lightning Source LLC
Chambersburg PA
CBHW030411310726
48979CB00002B/366

* 9 7 9 8 2 1 8 4 5 7 1 3 6 *